You're Abo... W9-CNV-061

Privileged Woman.

INTRODUCING
PAGES & PRIVILEGES™.

It's our way of thanking you for buying
our books at your favorite retail store.

GET ALL THIS FREE
WITH JUST ONE PROOF OF PURCHASE:

◆ **Hotel Discounts** up
to 60% at home and
abroad ◆ **Travel Service**
- Guaranteed lowest
published airfares
plus 5% cash back

$50 VALUE

on tickets ◆ **$25 Travel Voucher**

◆ **Sensuous Petite Parfumerie** collection

◆ **Insider Tips Letter**
with sneak previews
of upcoming books

You'll get a FREE personal card, too.
It's your passport to all these benefits– and to
even more great gifts & benefits to come!

There's no club to join. No purchase commitment. No obligation.

Enrollment Form

☐ *Yes!* I WANT TO BE A *Privileged Woman.*

Enclosed is one *PAGES & PRIVILEGES™* Proof of Purchase
from any Harlequin or Silhouette book currently for
sale in stores (Proofs of Purchase are found on
the back pages of books) and the store cash
register receipt. Please enroll me in *PAGES
& PRIVILEGES™*. Send my Welcome
Kit and FREE Gifts -- and activate my
FREE benefits -- immediately.

*More great gifts and benefits to come like these
luxurious Truly Lace and L'Effleur gift baskets.*

NAME (please print)

ADDRESS   APT. NO

CITY   STATE   ZIP/POSTAL CODE

PROOF OF PURCHASE   SAMPLE OF PURCHASE ONLY

Please allow 6-8 weeks for delivery. Quantities are
limited. We reserve the right to substitute items.
Enroll before October 31, 1995 and receive
one full year of benefits.

NO CLUB!
NO COMMITMENT!
*Just one purchase brings
you great Free Gifts
and Benefits!*
(More details in back of this book.)

Name of store where this book was purchased_____

Date of purchase_____

Type of store:

☐ Bookstore   ☐ Supermarket   ☐ Drugstore

☐ Dept. or discount store (e.g. K-Mart or Walmart)

☐ Other (specify)_____

Which Harlequin or Silhouette series do you usually read?

_____

Complete and mail with one Proof of Purchase and store receipt to:

U.S.: *PAGES & PRIVILEGES™*, P.O. Box 1960, Danbury, CT 06813-1960

Canada: *PAGES & PRIVILEGES™*, 49-6A The Donway West, P.O. 813,
North York, ON M3C 2E8   **PRINTED IN U.S.A**

"You Think Proposing Marriage Is A Solution?"

Meredith sighed. "We can't even be in the same room together for ten minutes without arguing. Do you think I want to raise my child in that kind of environment?"

"Our child," Logan replied. "And we'll change."

This woman was carrying his child. He'd resigned himself to the idea that a wife and children simply weren't in the cards for him. Now that it had happened, however, did she think he was going to let the opportunity slip through his fingers?

"You're going to marry me, Meredith," he said quietly.

"What if I decided to run away instead?"

He shook his head, pleased with the calmness he felt. "Your running days are over."

"But we're not in love!"

He leaned over her, bracing his hands on either side of her. "I want the baby, Meredith...and I want you."

Dear Reader,

Here at Desire, hot summer months mean even *hotter* reading, beginning with Joan Johnston's *The Disobedient Bride,* the next addition to her fabulous Children of Hawk's Way series—*and* July's *Man of the Month.*

Next up is *Falcon's Lair,* a sizzling love story by Sara Orwig, an author many of you already know— although she's new to Desire. And if you like family stories, don't miss Christine Rimmer's unforgettable *Cat's Cradle or* Caroline Cross's delightful *Operation Mommy.*

A book from award winner Helen R. Myers is always a treat, so I'm glad we have *The Rebel and the Hero* this month. And Diana Mars's many fans will be thrilled with *Mixed-up Matrimony.* If you like humor, you'll like this engaging—and *very* sensuous—love story.

Next month, there is much more to look forward to, including *The Wilde Bunch,* a *Man of the Month* by Barbara Boswell, and *Heart of the Hunter,* the first book in a new series by BJ James.

As always, your opinions are important to me. So continue to let me know what you like about Silhouette Desire!

Sincerely,

Lucia Macro
Senior Editor

Please address questions and book requests to:
Silhouette Reader Service
U.S.: 3010 Walden Ave., P.O. Box 1325, Buffalo, NY 14269
Canadian: P.O. Box 609, Fort Erie, Ont. L2A 5X3

HELEN R. MYERS

THE REBEL AND THE HERO

SILHOUETTE *Desire*

Published by Silhouette Books

America's Publisher of Contemporary Romance

If you purchased this book without a cover you should be aware that this book is stolen property. It was reported as "unsold and destroyed" to the publisher, and neither the author nor the publisher has received any payment for this "stripped book."

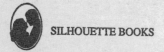

SILHOUETTE BOOKS

ISBN 0-373-05941-8

THE REBEL AND THE HERO

Copyright © 1995 by Helen R. Myers

All rights reserved. Except for use in any review, the reproduction or utilization of this work in whole or in part in any form by any electronic, mechanical or other means, now known or hereafter invented, including xerography, photocopying and recording, or in any information storage or retrieval system, is forbidden without the written permission of the editorial office, Silhouette Books, 300 East 42nd Street, New York, NY 10017 U.S.A.

All characters in this book have no existence outside the imagination of the author and have no relation whatsoever to anyone bearing the same name or names. They are not even distantly inspired by any individual known or unknown to the author, and all incidents are pure invention.

This edition published by arrangement with Harlequin Enterprises B.V.

® and TM are trademarks of Harlequin Enterprises B.V., used under license. Trademarks indicated with ® are registered in the United States Patent and Trademark Office, the Canadian Trade Marks Office and in other countries.

Printed in U.S.A.

HELEN R. MYERS

satisfies her preference for a reclusive life-style by living deep in the Piney Woods of East Texas with her husband, Robert, and—because they were there first—the various species of four-legged and winged creatures that wander throughout their ranch. To write has been her lifelong dream, and to bring a slightly different flavor to each book is an ongoing ambition.

Admittedly restless, she says that it helps her writing, explaining, "It makes me reach for new territory and experiment with old boundaries." In 1993 the Romance Writers of America awarded *Navarrone* the prestigious RITA for Best Short Contemporary Novel of the Year.

In loving memory of my uncle,
Peter R. Serpas, U.S. Army, Ret.
1920-1994

Prologue

Twenty-five years ago

Between the downpour and the late hour, Merri couldn't identify the person crossing Main Street and approaching the gas station, at least not clearly. But one glimpse of the man's confident, determined stride and intimidating silhouette and she knew immediately that he wasn't a customer. That didn't mean he wouldn't keep her from locking up the garage for Mr. Monroe, however; she understood that, just as she accepted how on another level she'd been expecting him. If the truth be known, she'd been preparing for this moment with the same stomach-churning anxiety for most of her young life.

As her heart began to pound and her hands grew clammy, she struggled against a final panicky urge to jerk down the overhead door. Better to face him in the light than to deal with him later, somewhere outside and in the dark, she assured herself.

But she did reach for the rag in the back pocket of her coveralls and wiped at the sweat covering her palms.

No one had ever made her more aware of being female than Logan Alan Powers. At the same time, no one had ever made her feel more incompetent at being a woman than he could with a mere glance. She feared him and his strange power, as much as she despised him for making her sensitive and vulnerable to it. To him.

As he stepped beneath the closest streetlamp, she noted that under his raincoat he still wore his dress uniform; yet he'd been home for—what? Hours. Why couldn't he have changed? The clothing made things worse, since the military garb emphasized a powerful build she didn't want to remember. And harsh, intensive boot camp training, followed by twelve months in Vietnam, had honed him further. To perfection. With every step he took, she grew more aware how much bigger he was physically than she was, even more so than she could recall. Now his shoulders seemed almost as broad as the aging compact she'd been working on; his chest, too. The change accented a trim waist and the long legs that had won him fame as the best receiver in the history of Rachel, Louisiana, football.

Although the shiny black brim of his hat was tugged low, it couldn't hide eyes capable of impaling her through the darkness. Those eyes gave his angular face a mature, formidable look, instead of the simple bold, capable one of his youth. A man like Logan didn't need that kind of advantage, she thought with mounting resentment and edginess. It wasn't fair.

Yes, the changes increased her unease. What she'd feared most had come true; the army Logan had joined shortly after high school had clearly made him into a professional killing machine at twenty. If he'd been hard before, what chance did she have of reasoning with the man he'd become?

He slowed for the last few steps, and came to a stiff halt just under the protection of the overhang, a mere three feet away from her. Even the rain seemed eager to escape as it sluiced off him to puddle at his feet. His predator's eyes, brown and amber, were ever watchful and probing. They roamed over her face, then down her body, without giving away any emotion, before locking again with hers.

"Meredith."

She hated his stubborn use of her given name; knew he was aware that it made her cringe because she didn't feel it fit her reputation as the town's resident misfit and all-around rebel. Of course, neither did her nickname, Merri, which Brett had dubbed her the day she met the brothers. But at least Merri didn't suggest she should be reaching for something she could never be. No, she couldn't, wouldn't, let Logan get to her this time. Brett was counting on her to be strong.

"Well, well… If it isn't the conquering hero." Afraid he'd see her trembling hands, she crossed her arms over her chest, not caring if that did emphasize how nothing much had blossomed down there since they'd last met. Maybe he would forget that it had been a whole year since the night he'd plucked her out of his family's stock pond by the scruff of her neck. He hadn't seemed to give a darn then that she was as good as naked; surely he wouldn't care that her measurements hadn't improved since. "I heard you were back in town."

"For a while, anyway."

Despite their volatile history, the instant she heard that answer she felt more than she wanted to, and couldn't ignore the spasm of unease that gripped her middle. "What do you mean?'' she began, narrowing her eyes. "Don't tell me— No. You're not going back!"

He neither denied nor confirmed it. He simply stood there.

Frustrating man. His behavior was typical of him. Whenever he spoke, which wasn't often, she knew what he had to say would be no more explanatory than his enigmatic stares. This time, however, she wasn't about to let him intimidate or silence her.

"What's wrong with you, Logan? You've done your duty. Do you have a death wish or something?"

For a moment, he looked angry, and then...disappointed? No. She rejected her momentary confusion; it had to be fatigue that she'd noticed. Simple fatigue. A result of his having traveled all day. After all, why should Logan Powers be disappointed in her? You had to *care* to be disappointed, and Logan's concern stopped at his desire to keep her away from his younger brother. Stronger was his perverse fondness for making her miserable whenever their paths crossed—although she could never fathom why. But from the first day they met, when she was eight and he twelve, he'd enjoyed doing everything from scowling at the way she dressed to editing practically anything that came out of her mouth. And when that didn't work, he'd tried to deny her very existence. To this day, she couldn't decide what had upset her more.

"You're still too young to understand," he said, a strange flatness in his voice.

Uttering an unladylike snort, Merri tugged her baseball cap down more snugly on her head. "Maybe. But at least I don't go around acting like I know everything. And when it comes to something as stupid as war, I hope I never get old enough *to* understand."

A pickup rushed by and honked. Neither one of them acknowledged it. For her part, Merri couldn't have if she wanted to, because her impulsive outburst had once again made her a prisoner of Logan's unblinking stare. But no matter how foolish, how small, those riveting brown eyes made her feel, she intended not to cower this time. Nor to run away.

"That makes two of us, Squirt," he said at last. He released her from his hypnotic hold by glancing around the interior of the garage. "Why don't we drop the subject? Just tell me where he is."

"Who?"

"Don't play games with me, Meredith. Where's my brother?"

She swallowed, remembering that the lower and softer he spoke, the more dangerous his temper grew. "So you've heard."

"That his draft number's come up? Yeah."

"He doesn't want to go, Logan."

"I'm sure Uncle Sam would be crushed to hear that."

"I mean it."

"It's his duty."

Disgusted, she rolled her eyes. "Please. Some clown in Washington decides he's the Almighty, and thousands of young men have to leave their homes and families to—to maybe die in places with names they can't begin to pronounce? Give me a break."

The muscles along Logan's strong jaw flexed. "I'm not about to debate politics or morals with you, little girl. Besides not having the time, I don't have the stomach for it. All I want is to find Brett, and I know if anyone has an idea about where he is, you do. Lord knows you two've been as close as Siamese twins for longer than I care to remember."

Why did he have to make that sound less than complimentary? "It's called friendship," Merri snapped back at him. "Not that you'd know what that is. I don't ask Brett to be something he's not, and I understand what he needs. Right now, he needs to be left alone."

"Tough. He doesn't have the luxury of time. He has things to do before he leaves. And if he doesn't report in on schedule, I assure you the people who'll come looking for him will make me look like the tooth fairy. Now where is he? My mother said he vanished right after he read his mail. She's worried sick about him."

"She could have called me here. I would have reassured her."

"She doesn't want reassurances, she wants her youngest son back. Tonight. If you had anything close to a home life yourself, or any gratitude for all she's done for you, you'd feel some compassion for what she's going through."

Merri could feel the blood drain from her face, and she had to clench her hands into fists to keep from taking a swing at him. "That's a lousy thing to say. You know I care for your mother more than— Damn you, Logan!"

She spun away, fighting the painful knot that blocked the rest of what she wanted to say. It was no secret that she'd been born out of wedlock, and that her mother—who currently worked nights as a cocktail waitress at Smokey's Lounge—spent more time in strangers' beds than her own. Logan had been cruel to remind her that she was nothing, trash, compared to his family, compared to most of the families in Rachel.

When she felt his hand on her shoulder, she tried to shrug it off. But she knew nothing short of a bullet would stop Logan from getting his way. As expected, he had no trouble forcing her to face him again.

"Stop squirming, Little Bit. And try to forget I said that. I guess I'm more tired from that bus trip up from New Orleans than I thought. At any rate, I didn't mean it. Not in the way you think."

That was a laugh. "You never say anything you don't mean. And stop calling me those stupid names. For your information, I'm not a kid anymore!" She dragged her hat off her head so that he could better see that, although her hair remained dramatically short compared to the way other girls were wearing theirs, she proudly wore the sapphire stud earrings Brett had given her as an early birthday present. They weren't her birthstone; he said he'd picked them because they matched her eyes. She liked them for the way they made her look. Older. Seventeen, at least. "I'll be sixteen the end of this week," she added with a proud tilt of her head.

Logan twisted his lips in what might have been a smile, if not for the downturned corners. "Couldn't tell by looking at you. You're still not much bigger than my thumb. Two of you could fit in those coveralls, and if your hair gets any shorter, someone may think you belong in boot camp, too."

As he spoke, he reached out and tousled her short locks. His touch wasn't unkind, but Merri was too angry not to slap his hand away.

"Do you mind? You may think I'm wet behind the ears, but Brett doesn't. He appreciates me for who and what I am, and *his* is the only opinion that matters."

The fleeting humor vanished from Logan's eyes. "Is that so? Exactly how serious have things become between you two? You aren't getting into any trouble, are you?"

His intonation left no doubt as to what he meant, and Merri could feel the heat of embarrassment rise up her neck and sting her cheeks. "Of course not! But if we were, it wouldn't be any business of yours."

"Think again," he replied, scowling. "A few years in the service will straighten him out."

Merri wasn't about to stand for talk like that. "He doesn't need straightening out!"

"Anyone that loses his head over a baby like you does."

"Go ahead and insult me, but it won't change anything. Brett's different. He's ... well, he's brilliant."

"Brilliant, my butt. That young fool couldn't survive on his own for a week, let alone support a wife and family."

"There's more to life than money," she countered, proud that she understood Brett's talents and dreams better than his brother ever had. "He's a talented artist and a poet. Someday he's going to have his own studio, where he'll share himself with people who appreciate how gifted he is."

"Right," Logan muttered, his expression mirroring his scorn. "A lot of good that'll do him in the real world."

"What real world, Logan? *Yours?*" Aware her emotions were getting the best of her, but unable to stop the flood of words, Merri gripped her hat tightly. "He's not a—a warmonger. He'd die if you asked him to do what you do... what you find so easy. He'd die. In here," she whispered, thumping her chest.

"Easy?"

"You know what I mean, Logan."

His gaze fell to where her hand rested. When he lifted his eyes to her face again, they lingered on her mouth and something less angry, but no less disturbing glittered in them. "Maybe I do. And maybe you are growing up faster than I thought."

She didn't know what to make of that look, or the gruffer tone in his voice, and so she opted for suspicion. "That's what I told you."

"Yeah, you told me. Now let me tell you something, Wildcat. Don't make the mistake of believing Brett will ever be enough for you. You'll end up disappointed."

His hot, angry words washed over her like steam from a doused fire. "How can you say that about your own brother?" she cried, aghast.

His chest rose and fell on a deep sigh. "Believe me, it isn't easy. Now where is he?"

She knew she'd delayed him as long as she could, yet a quick glance over her shoulder told her that Mr. Monroe still remained on the phone, back in his office. She couldn't leave for the day before checking with him. That meant she had to buy time. But the only way she could think to do so was by inciting Logan further and hopefully making *him* leave. "I'm not going to tell you."

"You'd prefer I force it out of you?"

Her heart began pounding with a new tension that she felt in every pulse point of her body. "You couldn't."

Rather than answer, he took a step toward her. Merri had never seen such a look of fearless intent before. It made those times when they were young—when both she and Brett had fled from him the way Mrs. Powers's chickens scrambled to escape their mean barnyard cat—seem like child's play in comparison.

Deciding her neck was more important than her job, she tried to sidestep him and run. But Logan had become faster than she remembered. In the space of a heartbeat, he had her imprisoned in the viselike grip of his arms.

Acting brave proved difficult, especially with nothing more substantial than air beneath her feet; nevertheless, she tried. Nose to nose with him, she matched him glare for glare.

"One of these days you're going to learn there are times when it's smarter not to push your luck," he told her slowly, his voice as dark as the sky behind him. "Not to push it with anyone, but most of all with me."

She could barely concentrate on what he was saying. Being trapped and plastered against him like this was doing more than soaking her, it was forcing her to feel his power and strength, despite the multiple layers of his clothes and hers. It made her aware of herself in a way all the sweet kisses she'd shared with Brett hadn't, and *that* revelation terrified as much as fascinated her.

Holding fast to what remained of her sanity, she managed, "I'm not afraid of you, Logan. Bully all you want, but it won't do you any good."

"Who said anything about bullying you?" he murmured, frowning as he slid his gaze over her face and once again let it rest on her mouth.

Merri felt the look in the most shameful places. But as decadent as those feelings seemed, a part of her wanted him to take control, to commit the unspeakable. She wanted to taunt him into doing what she saw he was suddenly, finally, thinking about doing. She couldn't have explained why if her life depended on it—except that she knew his kiss would feel like nothing she'd ever experienced before, and she wanted to carry the memory in her heart. Always.

Could her mother be right? Would she end up just like her, after all? Loose, needy...insatiable?

Logan began lowering his head. She could feel his heat as he inched his mouth nearer to hers . . . and nearer. Suddenly fear, sheer terror, took control.

"No," she whispered, pushing desperately against his chest. "Oh, Logan, wait! *Don't!*"

He blinked as though coming out of a trance, then swore. An instant later, he set her on her feet and took a step backward. Merri used the opportunity to run.

She raced out into the night, oblivious of the intensifying downpour. She had to find Brett. It no longer mattered if Mr. Monroe got angry at her for leaving without permission. She had to reach Brett and tell him their plans had to be changed. They had to leave tonight.

"Meredith!"

She wouldn't listen. She wouldn't.

"Merri!"

His cry almost stopped her. The sound of her name on his lips, his desperation... She felt herself momentarily doubting, reconsidering everything. She'd never heard such... What was it? There'd been undeniable grief and pain in his voice, yes. But something else, too.

It doesn't matter. This isn't just about you! Brett needs you.

She nearly stumbled, but she recovered quickly and pressed onward. Yes, they had to go tonight, she thought, her mind clearing, focusing. Because something she couldn't, didn't dare, deal with had just happened. Brett need never know. She would never tell him. But it was horrifyingly clear that he wasn't the only one who needed to run.

One

Twenty-five years later

Between the downpour and the late hour, Merri couldn't identify the person walking toward her, but she would have recognized the man's confident stride and intimidating silhouette anywhere. Even after all these years.

Just as in the old days, he triggered instincts of self-preservation and made her want to run. But she wouldn't, not this time. She was past running, having left her childhood far behind her; and she intended to prove to herself that she could stand up to Logan, if only to fulfill a promise to herself.

But, oh, he was angry. She saw it in the taut line of his broad shoulders, and the forward thrust of his head as he walked. In fact, he looked ready to charge. She had hoped that twenty-five years, and countless miles between them, had mellowed him, but apparently he carried enough anger and bitterness inside him to last a lifetime.

She should never have come back out here, or at least she should have waited until daylight. The cemetery wasn't a place for a scene. But she'd attended this morning's hasty private service for Faith's and Danny's sakes, fully aware that she would need this quiet time to say goodbye. Besides, she loved being out in the rain. Good thing, too, since it was coming down in torrents. Every stitch of clothing, from her denim jacket and jeans inward, was drenched. This soaker was warm, though, not like the last time she and Logan had come face-to-face. It was May, not September, and the rain was typical of central Louisiana's spring showers, although without the violence of lightning and thunder. Thank goodness for that, too, she thought dryly; there was more than enough electricity crackling in the few yards separating her and her brother-in-law.

Resigned to waiting for the worst, Merri lowered her gaze to the spray of fresh flowers covering the new grave. The sad part about the weather was that the heavy raindrops were crushing the sturdier blossoms and shredding the more fragile ones. The effect resembled the condition of her heart.

"You never did have the sense of a five-year-old."

She didn't bother looking up. Instead, she thought how odd it was to remember his voice so perfectly. Deep and rumbling, it suited the weather. But she also knew that the more agitated he became, the more clipped and harsh it would sound. She had every confidence she would soon be thoroughly reacquainted with *that* sound, as well.

"Hello to you, too, Logan. Nice of you to finally show up. I'm sure Brett's touched."

She could feel the stormy emotions emanating from him, and she knew he would as soon throttle her for that smart-alecky response as talk. So much for promising herself to turn over a new leaf. Of course, she had never professed to being a saint.

"Missing the funeral couldn't be helped," Logan said, stiffly. "Something came up, and I couldn't get back in time."

Reluctant though she was, Merri looked up from the grave that separated them. She didn't bother attempting to stop the disparaging laugh that rose in her throat like burning lava. "You build houses, Logan. That's not exactly on par with neurosurgery. I mean—" as usual when she grew emotional, she had to grope for the right words "—even the president puts the problems of the country on hold to watch a movie with his daughter. What could possibly have been so important that it couldn't wait?"

Despite his rain-soaked sport jacket and muddied dress slacks, he managed to maintain an authoritative and indignant manner. "I was aware my mother had been keeping in touch with you, but I had no idea how thoroughly she'd filled you in on the details of our lives."

"Don't worry," Merri snapped back, so angry she wondered if steam would soon begin rising from her. She curled the hands in her pockets into fists; it seemed the smarter thing to do, although heaven knew she was tempted by a more violent impulse. "We preferred discussing things like canning and recipes, not sorting through your private life or analyzing the financial condition of your company."

"If you say so."

"For heaven's sake, Logan, so she mentioned you once in a while. Who should she have talked about? We're family. Brett was your brother!"

"Don't remind me."

What a terrible thing to say, especially considering where they stood. Merri shook her head at the glowering giant, dismayed at how nothing had changed. "To think I believed you might have learned something in all these years. What a fool I was to hope that time, *life,* would have turned you into a . . . a human being like the rest of us.''

She spun around, determined not to taint this peaceful place with further outbursts, or bitterness. Logan could stay and sulk, or do what he would. She'd had enough.

As she walked, the saturated ground yielded like soft dough, despite her slight weight; the slick grass made each step as treacherous as ice. She almost lost her balance several times. As a result, Logan had no problem catching up with her.

Still a good distance from the station wagon she'd borrowed from her mother-in-law, she felt his viselike grip close around her wrist. Just like old times, she thought dizzily as he swung her around to face him. She couldn't help but wince at the stinging bite of all ten fingers when he shifted his hold to her upper arms.

''Take your hands off me!''

Not caring that she was half blinded by the rain pouring into her eyes, she glared up at the man who had intruded into her dreams more often than she cared to remember, and turned them into hauntings. Although the cemetery's security lights weren't at their most effective back here, she saw that time hadn't done her a favor and cut him down to her size. He looked bigger than ever, and stronger, too, which made her guess that his construction company was more of a hands-on operation than his attire might suggest. Demanding, as well, she thought, noting a generous amount of gray beginning to streak through his dark brown hair. What was more, deeper, almost craggy lines were remapping his face, altering territory they'd laid siege to long ago, when he'd earned his scar.

She settled her gaze on the diagonal slash bisecting his squared chin. Pale against his otherwise wind- and sun-bronzed skin, it was a souvenir from his second tour in Vietnam, the time he'd earned a Purple Heart to go with his Silver Star. Faith had written to her about that incident, too. Seeing it for the first time made Merri feel queasy in her stomach, and she had to look away.

"It ruined my photogenic face, didn't it?"

He'd never been close to handsome, and he knew it. But Merri had always believed he possessed something more than cover-model-perfect men did; he'd always had strength and character in his face that drew the eye. He still did, but the scar made it all the more dramatic. "I looked away because I was saddened at the thought of what you'd been through, not because of how it looks."

"Sure you did."

There was no sense trying to explain to him. He believed what he wanted to believe. He always had. "Let me go."

"As soon as we get a few things straight."

Not when his voice was as cold as she was beginning to feel. "I don't think we have anything else to say to each other."

"Good. We'll get done sooner if you keep your mouth shut."

"You ... Oh, you're still an insufferable jerk!"

"And you're a spoiled brat!"

She stopped trying to wrestle free and stared. She couldn't believe he'd said that.

"What's the matter? Don't tell me no one's ever called you that. Someone damn well should have."

She found the statement so ridiculous she almost laughed. Practically everyone in Rachel had known that she'd virtually raised herself. Year after year she'd been lucky if her mother remembered to buy her a new pair of shoes before school started, and maybe an outfit or two; she'd barely thought of the staples, like food. Most of the time Merri had been left to cope on her own. Something as simple as fresh milk had been an unknown commodity in the dilapidated shack they lived in. If it hadn't been for her few friends, like Brett, his mother, and Mr. Monroe, she might never have survived. By her definition, that made her anything but spoiled.

"You had Brett wrapped around your little finger from the day he met you," Logan continued as though reading her mind.

As her stunned reaction waned, she slowly shook her head. It had been Brett who did the charming. "We just became friends quickly. You never liked that, let alone understood it."

"A friend doesn't con another friend. You made him believe you were an innocent in dire need of guardianship and protection. The fact is, you saw an easy mark in him, and set him up. He was your way out of Rachel. Your path to a new life."

Good grief, the man enjoyed his bitterness. Small wonder his own marriage had ended in divorce. "Have it all figured out, do you?"

"Not all of it, but enough to know that about the time he realized he loved you, you'd filled his head with all that hippie ideological garbage."

Although he'd conveniently jumped a few years in his version of the past, Merri had no problem following him. "What garbage? The idea that killing is wrong? Sorry, I can't take credit for that one. Or maybe it was the idea that invading another country and ripping it apart wasn't progressive? I didn't have to put that notion in his head, either. Miracle of miracles, he'd figured it out all by himself."

Logan shook his head. "No one in their right mind likes war. But you're the one who supported Brett's idea of becoming a draft dodger and running away to Canada the moment he received his notice. My brother rarely faced up to his responsibilities, but he never flat-out ran away from them—that is, until he met you."

"That's not fair!" Merri cried, resuming her attempts to free herself. Once again she failed. "He hated fighting! He went along with you when you and your friends played war games or later got into skirmishes with other kids because he didn't want to disappoint *you*. But as he got older, it became harder and harder for him to keep up pretenses. He couldn't live in your shadow, Logan. He was different, and he realized that no matter how much you wanted it, it was wrong for him to try to be a smaller replica of you.

"Maybe you don't want to believe it, but it was his decision to leave," she concluded, remembering how painful that had been for Brett. "And I tried to warn you that it was coming before you left for your first tour. You wouldn't listen."

His eyes darkened and narrowed, and the corners of his mouth inched downward. "You didn't try too damned hard. And if you remember correctly, when I did get back to the States, you ran away from me."

For good reason. As she stared up into his angry face, she saw his gaze drift down to her mouth—just like the last time, that one time—and knew his own memories were rushing back with a vengeance.

No, she thought, fighting the assault of emotions that slammed into her like a heat wave and knocked the very breath out of her lungs. This couldn't happen again. Over the years, she'd convinced herself that it had all been a fluke; she didn't want to deal with the notion that after two and a half decades they could reexperience this same impossible reaction, be this vulnerable to each other. She detested him. He despised her. Good grief—in a few months she would be forty-one. She had a son who was about to

turn fifteen. Her husband hadn't been dead a week! She had
no business feeling this way. For pity's sake, the man was
her brother-in-law!

Logan recovered first, recoiling as though he'd touched
a live electrical wire. Without a word, he spun around and
walked away into the darkness, his stride as long and determined as when he'd arrived.

Merri watched him until the night and the rain all but
veiled him from her view. Then she waited a bit longer, listening for the sound of a car door slamming, an engine
starting. When it didn't happen, she didn't know what to
think. Had she imagined the entire nerve-racking scene?

She cast a final apologetic glance toward the grave. This
wasn't at all what she'd had in mind for Brett's homecoming.

Crazy. He had to have been crazy to do what he'd just
done. He was nuts to have come out here at all. Once he
spotted his mother's car and realized who else he would find
here, he should have shifted into reverse and gotten the hell
out. He'd known he couldn't keep a grip on his anger and
bitterness around her; it'd had too many years to strengthen
and grow, until, like some virus, it had taken control of his
mind, consumed him.

If he wasn't careful, it would destroy him. *She* would.

He sat in his black extended-cab pickup truck on the far
side of the cemetery and stared out at nothing. Thanks to the
rain and the darkness, the windshield had turned his world
into an opaque screen. The steady downpour also helped
mute the pounding of his own blood pulsating in his ears.

So many years. So much disappointment and frustration. To have it all come down to this sense of continued
hopelessness, a feeling of being trapped in a state of limbo.
He hated it. He was a man of action; when a situation

needed resolving, when a problem arose, he dealt with it. He couldn't go through this insanity again. Damn her. Damn Brett for dying. Damn them both for coming back.

As he'd told Meredith, he'd known of her correspondence with his mother since two years after Meredith and Brett had run away. He remembered the date because it had been about when Meredith turned eighteen and parental permission no longer was an issue to keep her and Brett from marrying. Back then—still recovering from his second year in Vietnam, raw-nerved and spiritually wasted—he'd told his mother that while he couldn't stop her from writing, he didn't want to hear anything about what was inside those envelopes. As far as he was concerned, he'd insisted, his brother was dead, and for that matter, so was Meredith.

Although deeply disappointed, his mother had honored his request. In fact, she'd broken her word only twice—once several years later, to let him know he'd become an uncle, and the second time last Friday, after she'd received the news that Brett had lost a brief but fatal bout with cancer.

Logan pinched the bridge of his nose and fought the swell of complicated feelings that threatened to drown him. Gone. His baby brother dead. Brett had only been forty-three, for crying out loud. Two years his junior. The entire family had always been robust and healthy; why, he and Brett combined probably hadn't missed more than a dozen days of classes through their entire school years.

He sucked in a deep breath. No, he couldn't let himself feel so much. Brett had made his choices, and they had been the wrong ones. As far as he was concerned, the man buried in the family plot, two places away from his father, was a stranger.

How could two people who'd once been so close grow up to be polar opposites? To this day, Logan remained completely befuddled about it, and now that Meredith had done what his mother had asked and brought Brett home to rest, the memories refused to stay back where he'd thrust them.

He'd been two when Brett was born. Experts claimed children didn't remember much at that young age, but he could recollect vague memories of climbing out of his bed in the mornings and toddling to his old crib, where he'd stared with curiosity at the tiny person in there. How soon afterward had he begun defining what the word *brother* meant to him? A year later? Two?

Ultimately he'd found a definition—one that seemed to amuse and finally annoy his younger sibling. Although Brett had eventually learned to alternately take advantage of and resent him for it, Logan had lived by its code until Brett rebelled completely, choosing Meredith over his own flesh and blood, and Canada over the country of his birth.

What had gone wrong? Where had he failed him? How often he'd wished that their father had lived longer. He hadn't asked for this responsibility. But their career-soldier parent had died in a training accident shortly after Korea, and it had been left to Logan to see that Brett got the masculine guidance he needed. He'd tried as best as he could, as best he knew how, considering his limited experience, and despite their squabbles and disappointments, he'd allowed himself to believe that he was doing a fair job. Then Meredith had come along like some combination of headstrong stray puppy and winsome waif, and he'd known, even at the ripe old age of twelve, that he'd lost his brother forever.

Merri. Just the thought of her nickname made him do a slow boil. At eight, she'd already defied true definition. She'd been a law unto herself. That had grated on him, sometimes irrationally so. He'd insisted that her strange way of dressing wasn't "cute," as others seemed to think, her free-spirited behavior wasn't "refreshing," and her outrageous mouth definitely didn't spew out "absolute honesty." In fact, for the longest time Logan had seen her as a particularly annoying wood splinter in his life—certainly not big enough to be of serious consequence, but irritating nonetheless. Then she'd grown up, and he'd been left *really* wondering.

He was still wondering. Especially now, when—having convinced himself that the chemistry on that rainy, miserable night over two decades ago had been an aberration, an overflow of adrenaline—he suddenly found himself once again nearly undone by it.

Heaven help him. How could he go home with her there? He doubted he would get ten minutes of rest sleeping under the same roof. But he'd put his mother through too much already because of his absence during the burial. He had to go back.

Maybe he could get through it by reminding himself that Meredith would be leaving soon. It wasn't much to cling to, but it would have to do.

"My word, child, you're soaked through and through!"

Merri gave her mother-in-law a lopsided smile as she finished slipping off her soggy moccasins and draped her drenched jacket over the dryer. "Sorry for the mess!" she called back, peeking into the kitchen.

"Never mind that. Why do you think I had the washer and dryer put out in that entryway cubbyhole?" Faith's question ended with a sigh. "With two boys, and the farm work, I knew I'd be up all hours running myself ragged if I didn't arrange things to where you could leave the dirt as close to its natural place as possible." She lit a flame beneath the teakettle she'd just filled, then came to offer assistance. "The important thing is to get you dried off and warm as soon as possible. Worn-out as you are from your long journey, you have to watch not to catch a chill. Pneumonia can set in during this warm weather, too, you know."

"I'll dash upstairs and change as soon as I towel off."

Faith wagged a sturdy finger, but her broad, makeup-free face reflected nothing but affection and concern. "You'll do no such thing. Behind you in that closet is a terry-cloth robe I use when I get caught out in the weather. It's likely to be miles too big for you, but strip off and slip it on. That way we can toss your things into the washer here and now."

How like her, Merri thought with a new surge of gratitude. No questions about where she'd been, no recriminations; only the compassionate but solid logic of a woman who was too pragmatic to succumb to weaker emotions.

Nodding, she abruptly turned away and drew out the navy blue robe, appreciation getting the better of embarrassment. If it weren't for Faith, she would be on a bus heading back to Canada this very minute, now that their mission was accomplished, her word to her mother-in-law kept.

"Is Danny in bed?" she asked over her shoulder, once she knew she had control of her voice. She squirmed out of the shirt that wanted to stay glued to her back and arms.

"About twenty minutes ago. He'd been fighting his fatigue for a while, until I couldn't stand watching anymore and bullied him upstairs. Grumbled at me all the way, he did, but he went out like a light the minute he pulled the sheet under his chin." Wise, slightly myopic eyes grew tender. "He's a wonderful boy, dear. You should be proud of the fine job you did raising him."

Merri nodded her thanks, but ducked her head, pretending to concentrate on unzipping her jeans. Few things got to her faster than praise about her son. He was her heart.

"You know, I'd forgotten how much it rains here in the spring," she said, once she swallowed this latest lump in her throat.

Faith emptied the coins and keys from the jacket pockets onto the dryer, then dumped the jacket and Merri's shirt into the filling tub of soapy water. "It's been wetter than usual this year. Of course, the whole country seems to be topsy-turvy weatherwise." Suddenly she gasped. "Mercy, child!"

Startled, Merri turned around. "What?"

"You're thinner than ranch wire!"

Although Merri had stripped down to nothing more than a pair of soggy cotton briefs, being stared at didn't phase her. In fact, amused at the other woman's shock, she replied, "I'm only five-three, Faith." She cast her a wry glance as she reached for the robe. "I couldn't comfortably carry much weight. When I was pregnant with Danny, I only gained sixteen pounds, and even with that I thought my back was going to snap from the strain."

Faith was several inches taller, with a far more solid bone structure, and her fragility showed only through her gray-velvet eyes. "Oh, Merri . . . I'm ashamed to say it, but I'm glad you never told me that. I would have rushed up there, meddling and bossing you without mercy."

That might have been rather nice. Merri had never been coddled by anyone before, except Brett. Sometimes. When he hadn't been deep in some creative fog.

"You have my blessing to turn all that energy and concern toward Danny," she told her, tying the robe's thick belt. "I could use the relief, since fate decided to have a bit of fun by giving me a son who's already two inches taller than me, and likes to act as if he's twice my age. It might help to counter that with a grandmother's influence to keep him from overdoing it and forgetting to enjoy his youth."

Faith added Merri's jeans to the other clothes in the washer and closed the lid. "Don't you worry. I already have plans." She clucked her tongue. "Still can't get over how much he favors Brett. Goes all the way down to his mannerisms. Have you noticed?"

"Oh, yes." And maybe that was just as well, Merri thought, thinking about her deplorable behavior at the cemetery. She certainly didn't want him inheriting her temper!

Something in her expression must have betrayed her thoughts because after stretching her damp socks on the dryer, Faith put an arm around Merri's shoulders and led her into the kitchen. "I wasn't going to ask—a person needs their privacy—but are you all right? When you said you needed some air...well, I couldn't help but wonder. Mind you, I was glad to lend you the car."

Merri slipped her arm around her mother-in-law's pleasantly plump waist. "I know. I appreciate it, too." Aware the truth was bound to come out sooner or later, she decided to confess. "I went back to the cemetery."

"Ah. I guessed as much."

"It's not that this morning's quiet burial wasn't lovely. I can't tell you how grateful I am that you arranged everything to be ready the hour we arrived. I guess because it was over so fast, I needed another while to be there by myself."

"You don't owe me any explanation."

"But I want you to know I appreciate you tolerating my eccentricity. Brett was such a huge part of my life," Merri continued, her head spinning from all the thoughts and experiences she hadn't been able to share with anyone over the years. Granted, there had been the wonderful letters she'd exchanged with Faith, but there were things you didn't tell your husband's mother.

After urging her to sit down at one of the four red vinyl dinette chairs, Faith returned to the stove and poured the boiling water into the two mugs she'd set out. "I understand. Life is complicated all by itself. Marriage makes it more so. When you lose your life's mate..." She paid just a bit too much attention to adjusting the slipping tea bag in the left mug. "If you ever need to talk about anything, I want you to know that I'm here for you."

No. There were things that not only wouldn't be fair, they'd be painful to bring up. Faith had missed so much of the good moments in Brett's life, Merri couldn't expose her to any of the rest.

"He may have been my son, Merri, but don't forget, you're my daughter. That's the truth, every bit as much as if I'd given birth to you myself."

No one had ever said anything kinder to her. In fact, her own mother, who'd died several years ago in some run-down motel near the Mexican border, had never managed anything close. It again brought home how special this woman was to her, and it resurrected Merri's concern about losing her friendship.

"I'm going to doctor this tea for you," Faith continued, with another dose of maternal concern. "My own special recipe for when you're physically and emotionally worn-out. After you've finished all of it, you're going upstairs for a nice hot shower, and—"

"Faith. I have to tell you...Logan showed up."

Faith's short gray hair gleamed with flashes of silver as she jerked her head up. Understandably, surprise left her momentarily speechless. When she recovered, she adjusted the small silver cross in the neckline of her floral-print smock. "Did he say what happened this morning? Is he all right? Where is he now?"

They were legitimate questions, but Merri didn't know how to begin answering them. "I don't know. He said something about having had some problems, but...he didn't explain." She lowered her eyes, regretting the reason behind Logan's uncommunicativeness. Somehow she had to prepare her mother-in-law for the worst. "I'm pretty sure it's my fault, though. You know how he feels about me."

"Yes, but I can't say I understand it, let alone respect him for it." Faith rubbed eyes that had been red-rimmed all day. "He warned me that if I went through with my idea of bringing you all back, he would make himself scarce. We had words over it, but I didn't think he meant to carry through with the threat." She shot Merri a hopeful glance. "Did he at least hint if he's coming home tonight?"

Merri wished she could give the answer she knew Faith wanted, but it would have been a lie. "No. He became so angry with me that he left before I did. I'm sorry, Faith. I blew it, and I take full responsibility."

The woman pursed her lips and shook her head. "From the first day Brett brought you home from school and asked if you could stay for supper, Logan's acted as if you had the rabies, or worse." She smiled sadly. "Truth is, Brett did take to you the way he did those small critters he was always finding in the fields, or by some creek. But that doesn't ex-plain or excuse Logan's behaving the way he does, and I'll tell you this . . . it's time it stopped."

That kind of talk only deepened Merri's dread. "He's a grown man, Faith. He has a right to his opinions."

"At least that's something we can agree on."

The noise from the washing machine had blocked out the sound of the back door opening, but Merri turned in time to catch Logan's grim expression as he filled the entryway as only he could. He, too, was dripping wet; however, that didn't stop him from coming straight into the kitchen.

In the fluorescent light, she had a better view of the ef-fects of time and bitterness on him. The gray in his hair was more widespread than she'd first thought, the scar on his chin more brutal. But most of all, she noted as his gaze settled on her, she'd never seen such a warm color of eyes look so hard and unforgiving.

"Logan, this is still my house," Faith snapped, breaking into the uneasy silence. "Don't shame me by forgetting that. You've already hurt me enough by not showing up for your brother's burial."

His gaze never shifted off Merri. "My brother died twenty-five years ago."

"Logan!"

Merri winced, but more at the anguish in Faith's cry than for Logan's cruel words. Barely checking her anger, she crossed her arms and drawled, "Fine job, bro. Nothing like making full use of that military training. Go straight for the jugular, and leave no one unmaimed."

His answering look could have drilled through steel. "This is none of your business. Stay out of it."

"That's enough," Faith declared, her bearing as rigid as her son's. "Logan, no mother deserves to be shamed by her child twice in one day, but you've managed it. You'd best know right now that Merri and Danny have accepted my invitation to stay on here with us."

"What did you say?" For the first time, he didn't look quite so arrogant, or in control.

Faith remained stoic, a steely Madonna matching him glare for glare. "You heard me. And it's not a matter that's up for discussion. You work around the clock these days, and Sherman manages this farm well enough without me breathing down his neck. What's left for me to do except some gardening, canning and such? I'm lonely. I want to reacquaint myself with the rest of my family before I get too feebleminded to know who they've grown up to be. So you'll behave, my boy, or you'll be the one to leave."

Despite looking a bit startled at her own bravery, she recovered quickly. Adding a sharp nod, Faith stalked out of the room.

Bewildered and dismayed, Merri used the steeping tea as an excuse to fidget. She hurried to the counter and lifted the bags out of both mugs and set them in the sink. After that, she stood feeling totally out of place. She didn't know where anything was yet, and she hadn't a clue as to what Faith had planned when she mentioned "doctoring" the tea. Actually, she didn't want the stuff, or anything else, for that matter. She just wished she could escape to her room, bury her head under a pillow, and sleep for a week.

She glanced toward Logan. "If you want one of these—"

His quelling look spoke volumes, and he turned away to remove his jacket. "Don't waste your time. My mother might have a right to be upset with me, but that doesn't change anything else."

Exhausted from her long journey and furious with him for hurting Faith, Merri snatched up one of the soggy tea bags and flung it at his back. "For heaven's sake, it's been twenty-five years, Logan! Can't you let go? Can't you—"

She never got to finish. With a muttered oath, he swung around and after one long stride took hold of the robe's belt and jerked her toward him. He closed his free hand around her throat.

"Not another word," he rasped in warning. "Not one."

"*Logan.*"

His rough handling had loosened the robe, and between the opening belt and the robe's size, it was all Merri could do to keep the thing from slipping off her shoulders. As it was, she wasn't too successful, and she saw Logan's expression change, the muscles along his sharp cheekbones stretch tight.

He eased his hold on her throat...but only to move his thumb slowly, ever so slowly, up and down the taut tendons of her neck. Heartbeats later, his fingers trailed to the pulse pounding frantically at the hollow of her throat, then down...down...until they hesitated at the shallow valley where her heart beat its own merciless tattoo.

Her body came alive, shockingly, painfully alive. Desire flared to life and burned. She wanted...him...so badly.

Just when she knew his hot fingers were about to trespass beyond the soft cotton to where she ached, to where she hadn't been touched in months, he seemed to rouse from his stupor and jerked back his hand. A second later, he released her.

Expecting anger, she saw only defeat. That stunned her as much as the rest.

"Why couldn't you have stayed away?" he demanded in a raw whisper.

TWO

The question continued to echo in Logan's head through the night. As a result, the next morning he entered the kitchen in the gray light of dawn preoccupied, and not at all ready to find that someone else was up even earlier than he was.

He froze. *Brett?* He almost spoke aloud. But in the last instant a flash of clarity kept him from making a fool of himself.

The skinny teenager, wearing nothing more than rumpled jeans, stared back at him. His sleepy eyes and tousled hair confirmed he was barely awake. "Uh . . . hi. I was just getting myself some milk."

"No problem."

The kid was on the small side for his age, and yet he was at a point of growth where his muscle development hadn't caught up with his stretching bones. Logan watched as he placed the empty glass in the sink and stared back in equal bewilderment, wondering what to say next.

"Are you my uncle Logan?"

The title sounded foreign to him. "I guess I am. That makes you Danny...or is it Daniel?"

The teen looked embarrassed as he bowed his head, his shaggy, chestnut brown hair tumbling over his forehead and veiling his eyes. "My mom calls me Danny."

"But?"

"It seems kinda dumb when you're fifteen."

"What do you prefer?" Logan asked, once again grateful that his young years were behind him. Not that being an adult was any easier, but at least you stopped rushing birthdays by weeks and months.

"Dan. Dan's fine." He swept his hair back just enough to peer at Logan. "What do I call you?"

"Logan will do. I reckon you're old enough."

Logan hadn't intended anything by that, surely not to make points. Nevertheless, a blind man wouldn't have missed the pleasure in the youngster's eyes.

"Are you sure?"

"Why shouldn't I be?"

"Well...you're *you*," the kid replied with a one-shoulder shrug.

Logan finished slipping into the sport coat he'd brought downstairs with him. "What's that supposed to mean?" No sooner was the question voiced than he realized he didn't want an answer. "Look at it this way. You don't know me. I don't know you. If we met on the street, or you were asking me for a job, you would call me—"

"Mr. Powers."

Logan could have groaned when he heard Meredith's cool voice behind him. So another thing about her hadn't changed; she still moved like a shadow. He should have known that in one day she could learn to avoid the squeaking boards on the stairs—a feat he'd been unsuccessful in mastering for as long as he lived here.

A swift glance over his shoulder told him that she hadn't slept any better than he had. Dark shadows pooled under her eyes, and her short, waifish hairdo looked almost as tousled as her son's. But what had him retreating toward the opposite side of the kitchen was seeing that she'd come down apparently wearing nothing more than a man's black T-shirt. Maybe it did reach to midthigh and could have been concealing shorts, or maybe her son was used to seeing his mother waltzing around dressed provocatively, but *he* didn't like it one bit.

"Couldn't sleep?"

At first Logan thought she was talking to him, but he soon realized Meredith had addressed her son.

"I got thirsty. Can I get you something?"

Polite kid. Logan could feel something easy and genuine flow between mother and son. Funny how the camaraderie left him feeling like an outsider in his own home; however, he hardly felt like laughing.

"I think I need a gallon of coffee, and a dozen toothpicks to open my eyes. But I'll get it. The coffee, that is," Meredith said, casting Logan a tentative look. "Can I get you some?"

Their eye contact triggered needlelike prickling throughout his body, and he wondered at his ability to keep from giving away his awareness. When she broke the connection and continued on to the stove, he almost sighed with relief. "I have to go."

"Sure? It won't take more than a few minutes, and it is early."

"I said *no.*"

He'd overreacted. But considering the way last night had ended, could he do anything less around her? Damned woman. It hadn't been twenty-four hours yet, and already she had him behaving like a stranger to himself.

Aware that she and her son stood waiting for something—an apology, he realized—he started for the door. All he could manage was "I have to go." He couldn't apologize. Allowing his voice to expose that he was more weary than angry was the best he could do.

"It's great to finally meet you, sir," Danny called after him. "Maybe we'll get to talk later?"

Standing half in and half out of the doorway, Logan took his first breath of humid morning air. Without looking back, he nodded, but he gave no verbal commitment before drawing the door closed behind him and securing his escape.

He only admitted his disgust and shame as he made his way to his truck. To be afraid of a kid... What would be next? It was seeing the curiosity and admiration in the boy's eyes that had done it. Logan had an uneasy feeling that Danny had seen the photo and medals his grandmother insisted on displaying beside Brett and Merri's wedding picture. Of course, they were hard to miss, since she'd set them on a shelf by the front door like some shrine.

Could it be that the kid didn't share his parents' aversion to the military? Whatever. That didn't mean Logan wanted to get into rehashing the past with him.

Damn it, Meredith, he thought once he could see the house in his rearview mirror. *Do the right thing for both of our sakes. Get the hell out of here.*

"He doesn't like me, Mom."

Danny's comment made Merri ache for her son. Such an anguished deduction deserved a bear hug of reassurance.

But, aware that he was at an age when hugs and kisses from a relative were as welcome as being driven to school, or escorted to the doctor for a sports physical, she forced herself to simply fill the kettle with water. "That's not true, Tiger. He's simply struggling with all the changes, the way we all are."

It felt strange to be defending Logan, considering their history. On the other hand, she saw no reason why Danny needed to get caught up with her and her brother-in-law's problems. If he and his uncle failed to mesh, it should be due to their own lack of chemistry. Nothing else.

Returning to the stove, she set the flame on the burner. Only then did she give her son her full concentration. "As the saying goes, Logan's a law unto himself. If we stay, you'll have to deal with that truth."

"If?"

She grimaced at the slip, then asked herself what would be the use of hiding her thoughts? Last night she'd all but concluded that they couldn't possibly stay. However, even in the fragile light of dawn she could see that Danny was thrilled with the idea of living here. Because of Brett's wanderlust, as well as his inability to find agreeable work, they'd moved quite a bit throughout Danny's short life. Obviously her son had had enough. He'd certainly chosen a heck of a place to take a stand, though; logical for him, maybe, but it would prove a nightmare for her.

"What I meant to say was . . ." She almost cheered at the sound of footsteps on the stairs.

"My goodness, didn't anyone want to sleep late this morning?" Faith asked, sweeping into the room, her caftan wafting slightly with every step. She paused to kiss Merri, and then a sheepish Danny.

Merri found it easy to smile at the woman, whose blue-and-green outfit reminded her of a Tiffany lamp. "You know how it is. New beds and all that." She hoped her mother-in-law would buy the half-truth.

"I should have guessed." Faith added a pat on Danny's back as she crossed to the refrigerator. "It will get better, though. You'll see." Her expression grew less confident. "Where's Logan? I thought I'd heard him come down."

Merri exchanged glances with her son. "He left a minute ago."

"After coming home so late..." Faith's sleep-marked face reflected her disappointment. "It's because of what I said to him last night."

"I don't think so," Merri replied, trying to reassure her. "He said he had something pressing to do." She liked that Faith still believed that once she'd made her point, an issue was closed. She wished she could perfect that "no grudge" attitude herself. But she'd never seen life that simply, which was why they needed to talk. Soon. However, not in front of Danny. He didn't need his young life burdened with her and Logan's ancient conflicts. "It sounds to me as if he had a breakfast meeting."

Faith seemed relieved by the excuse. "Oh, yes...that's probably it. He doesn't always remember to tell me. With the construction business picking up again, he has so much on his mind. Well, sit down, you two. I've been so looking forward to cooking for someone who'll sit still for five minutes, you'll just have to humor me."

The opportunity to talk honestly with her mother-in-law came only after breakfast. Once Danny retreated back upstairs and the dishes were cleared away, Faith invited Merri to join her outside as she checked the progress of her garden. Intent on getting her decision off her chest, Merri accepted readily.

She wasn't prepared for the strong wave of nostalgia that gripped her as they stepped outside. Yesterday she'd been in an emotional fog, but as she examined the lush green landscape now, she was amazed at her deep sense of homecoming. Then again, she told herself, she should have known; as easy as it had been to say goodbye to Rachel, the Powerses' homestead had long been a place of sanctuary for her.

She eyed it now with growing fondness, and even a touch of amusement. She'd been given countless meals in the Depression-era two-story white house. She'd climbed the great oaks and magnolias surrounding it to toss nuts and pebbles at Brett's window. And beyond, to the left of the vegetable and flower garden, was the barn where she'd slept several times, when her mother brought home strange men who frightened her too much for her to stay under the same roof with them. The barn had served as a perfect hiding spot, until old Sherman ratted on her to Faith, who offered her a bed inside the house. That invitation had become an open-ended offer.

Yes, she'd felt safe here—if not welcomed by *all* the occupants. She felt safe now, but still not entirely welcome.

"It hasn't changed much, has it?" Faith asked when she noticed Merri's prolonged study.

"Not very...except to look more solid than ever." She gestured toward the fields where young soybean stalks already created a shimmering sea of green. "Sherman's taking good care of the place."

"He's afraid that if he slows down I might retire him. What he doesn't realize is that I wouldn't know how to manage without him now. Neither of my boys proved to have the calling to be a farmer. I guess I'd sell the place if Sherman didn't want to sharecrop for me any longer. I know Logan could handle the taxes easily enough, but I'd feel guilty letting him. Thank goodness Sherman believes old farmers don't quit.''

Merri laughed softly. Her introduction to the reed-thin black man had come when he caught her swiping an apple from his lunch in the fields. Although she'd resisted taking the ham-and-cheese sandwich, because it seemed the more serious offense, she'd been willing to bite his hand for that apple. However, once he heard how long it had been since she'd had a real meal, he'd done more than promise not to turn her over to the police—he'd insisted she take everything. He'd never said a word about it to Faith, either; not even later, when he found her sleeping in the barn.

''He has to be older than dirt,'' she said wryly. ''Wasn't he past forty when I had my first run-in with him?''

''Mmm ... He's seventy now.'' Faith slipped on gardening gloves that matched the denim jumpsuit she'd changed into just before coming out. ''And it really riles me that he looks five years younger than my own sixty-seven!''

''Oh, Faith.'' Merri shook her head at the teasing woman. ''You'll look marvelous at eighty.''

''You're good for my ego, dear. But I wasn't hinting for a compliment. It's not as if I'm searching for romance or anything.''

''Maybe not, but it's right in front of your face if you're interested.'' When her mother-in-law all but gawked, Merri threw back her head and laughed outright, delighted. ''You haven't noticed how your mailman looks at you?''

''Stan Shirley is a sweet man, of course. But when did you—?''

''Yesterday, after we got back from the cemetery. I watched from upstairs as you went out to the mailbox.'' At the time, Merri had thought it strange that Faith hadn't asked her or Danny to do that for her, because although the burial had been brief and private, Faith had been deeply affected. Chatting with the postman, who'd pulled up seconds later, seemed the last thing anyone would want to do. But Merri quickly realized there was more going on than had initially met the eye.

How she'd misjudged her mother-in-law. The red-haired man, burly and whiskered, had reached out to take Faith's hand in both of his. Since she was inside, she hadn't heard what was said, but there had been no missing the look of concern and tenderness on the gruff-looking mail carrier's face.

"I should have known it wouldn't take you long to pick up on that. You always were an observant one." Faith touched her hair self-consciously. "He wanted to come to the service. To be there with me. But I wouldn't let him. I've been keeping him at arm's length for such a long time, you'd think he would give up on me."

"Why have you been?"

"Mostly because I'm a coward."

"Excuse me? You're one of the bravest women I've ever met!"

"Not about this. Dear, he's five years younger than me!"

With a shrug, Merri tugged on the extra pair of gloves her mother-in-law had offered her. "So? Maybe five years matters when we're kids and the gaps in development are more obvious, but don't forget, those gaps shrink to nothing the older we get."

"I understand all that in theory, and there's not a month that goes by when some magazine doesn't have an article on the subject. But that doesn't keep me from making some foolish excuse every time he asks me out for dinner or a movie. I keep thinking about what people would say."

"Probably something about being happy that you're getting out and enjoying life."

"Well, I can tell you this, Logan wouldn't like it." Faith knelt on a gardening pad and frowned at a crowded patch of radishes. She began thinning out the two-leafed plants with almost brutal zest. "What I didn't tell you is that Stan is Jane's uncle."

"Ouch."

At the mention of Logan's ex-wife, Merri's curiosity got the best of her. The marriage had occurred almost twenty years ago—rather impulsively, Faith had noted in one of her letters—and ended less than three years later. "Irreconcilable differences" was the reason Logan had given his mother the day Jane quietly moved out.

"Wait a minute—I thought her maiden name was Morris," Merri asked, confused, when she remembered the detail.

"Stan's her mother's brother."

Merri wished she could ask more questions about the marriage, but she knew that wasn't the subject Faith needed to focus on. "Well, I still think it's your life to live as you want. Surely Logan wouldn't begrudge you a little happiness?"

Glancing across the row as Merri crouched down to attend to the row beside hers, Faith uttered a sigh filled with doubt. "At any rate, right now it's more important for me to see you and Danny get settled in. And to try to make Logan stop being such a stubborn fool about you."

Here we go, Merri thought, seeing the opening she'd been waiting for. "You may be asking too much. Faith..." She reached out to touch her mother-in-law's tanned forearm. "We can't stay."

"What! Of course you can. Why, having you move in is the only thing that's made Brett's passing bearable."

"Hearing you say that means the world to me," Merri admitted, "but Logan's not happy, and he has more of a right to be here than we do. I know I promised I would try to get along with him. I suppose I spoke without thinking clearly. It seems that we still can't be in the same room without rubbing each other the wrong way. I don't want you to have to deal with that, and I certainly don't want Danny to be exposed to it. Believe it or not, he thinks his mother is a fairly cheerful and positive-minded person."

"So do I, dear. Which is why I want you to at least try and give this situation a chance for a little while longer. From the looks of things, Danny is going to be the only grandchild I'll ever have. Please...don't let me miss the rest of his growing years."

Feeling her resolve slip, Merri began to grope for excuses. "But I don't have a job! I'm not sure when I'd be able to help with expenses, let alone pay rent."

"You're family. You don't worry about rent. As for work, you just lost a husband. Take a little time to decide what you want to do with the rest of your life."

What she wanted was to be able to look at Logan and not simultaneously want to clobber the man and feel his arms around her. The thought came so quickly that Merri didn't have time to be embarrassed. "Under one condition," she said, trying to keep from being a complete marshmallow. "If at any time you decide you were wrong, that it's not working out, I want you to feel free to tell me. And vice versa."

"That's fair enough." Faith gave her a wistful smile. "Now, why don't you appease this mother's insatiable curiosity and tell me more about who my son was as a man?"

Logan delayed going home for as long as possible. At least that was easy to do these days, what with the market keeping steady. He currently juggled three crews and a fourth, smaller group doing cleanup and detail work. When

Powers Construction built a house, or even the occasional commercial building, the client had the satisfaction of knowing that painstaking personal effort went into every step of construction, down to making sure a kitchen sink was polished and ready for a busy homemaker, and that no dropped nails, leftover insulation or any other remnants littered the yard or had been forgotten in a closet. But tonight was one of those nights when his employees had done their work too well.

At nine o'clock, with barely a hint of light remaining in the western sky, he finished inspecting the last home, on the south side of Rachel. Tomorrow the Williams family could close as planned, and by this time tomorrow night the handsome redbrick Tudor's windows would all be lit as they started moving in their belongings. It made Logan feel good to have tangible proof of a job well-done, to be part of someone's future. Oh, the Williamses would forget that they'd taken forever in choosing the chandeliers for the house, and that he'd cost them an extra delay of several days when he refused to accept a shipment of carpeting inferior to what the family expected. In two or three years, they might have to think twice to remember he'd been the one to build the place. But that was fine. *He* knew, and that gave him more satisfaction than whatever the company earned on the project.

At least he could say he had one part of his life in order, he thought as he reluctantly turned the truck toward home. Then he grimaced, because the word *order* echoed mockingly in his mind. No kidding, he had order in his life; he had no marriage, no children, and a damn sorry love life. But the business was solid and thriving. While that was more than many people had in a day and age when divorce and bankruptcy statistics' only competition came from those for transmissible diseases, it left him feeling annoyingly empty tonight. Bitter, too. All because his mother had disrupted the tiny oasis of peace he had etched out for himself by coaxing Meredith back.

The mere thought of his sister-in-law had her face materializing before his mind's eye, and he gripped the steering wheel more tightly. Nothing had changed; just as she had in the old days, she'd cast her spell and wrapped everyone around her little finger. He still didn't know how she'd managed it, and he resented her power to turn everything and everyone into sheer upheaval. Hell, he hadn't even been able to have a quiet cup of coffee in his own home this morning!

What was he going to do? Business demands had allowed him to put off thinking about the situation most of the day. Now that he was only two miles from the house, that luxury no longer existed.

If Meredith and her son stayed, could he continue living there? Probably not. But how could he move out? For the past twenty-five years, he'd been his mother's right arm. Yes, she managed to make her own way financially, between what she earned with the farm and her income from his father's military benefits. She didn't need his financial help, although it was always there for the asking. But his presence had given her the companionship and sense of family he knew she craved. Because he loved and respected her, he didn't want to sever their bond. The problem was that there would be damned little peace if he had to face Meredith day in and day out.

God, if only the minx had changed, grown fat and dull. But not her. She'd matured, yes; however, the body he remembered for the most part as boyish, with its sharp angles, had become willowy and graceful; the shrewd, sharp mind had clearly been disciplined to at least give the illusion of wisdom and understanding. She'd become a woman, a woman he knew he wouldn't agree with on most issues, but could incite a sensual, sexual response in him faster than anyone he'd ever known. Fate didn't play fair at all.

His headlights picked up a figure about two hundred yards ahead. Someone was walking along the road, and because traffic wasn't heavy way out here, especially at this time of night, he didn't have to guess too much about who it could be.

He braked and pushed the electric button to lower the passenger window. "What the hell are you doing?" he demanded, already feeling his blood pressure rising. "Don't you realize the risks you're taking out here alone and in the dark?"

She looked up at the sky as if asking for divine guidance before peering through the opened window. "I was hoping to get a minute to talk to you away from the house."

"Is something wrong?" he asked, immediately concerned that something might have happened to his mother.

Meredith's expression turned slightly mocking. "What's not wrong, Logan?"

He didn't need this. It had been a long day. He was hungry, and thirsty, and he yearned for a long shower. Couldn't he deal with at least one of those three cravings before being asked to start this next round of verbal combat with her?

He returned his gaze to the windshield. "Get in."

As soon as she slipped into the passenger seat, he pulled over to the grassy side of the road and shifted into park. But he still didn't turn to look at her. The woman was wearing nothing more than cutoff jeans and a crimson knit top that showed an annoying amount of skin, and whatever subtle curves she possessed. He had no intention of giving her the satisfaction of seeing his awareness and discomfort with it.

"Thank you, Logan. I didn't think you'd give me as much as a minute of your time."

"Well, you have it, but you'd better get to the point. That brush line may hide us from view of the house, but don't think for a moment that my mother isn't aware that you're not in the house."

Merri smiled briefly. "I know. Brett used to laugh over the times he thought he'd slipped something past her—like sneaking me a bowl of the potato salad she'd made for the church's fellowship dinner—only to learn later, through her letters, that she'd known all the time."

"I'm not interested in sitting here and reminiscing about your intimate conversations with your husband. If that's what this little visit was all about, you wasted your time."

"You know it's not," she replied, tension in her voice again. As if she'd heard it herself, she cleared her throat and added, "I came out here to ask if we could call a truce."

A typical female tactic; as if the whole decision were up to him. What would be his was the blame if her idea didn't work. He shot her a skeptical look. "You think that's possible?"

"I don't know. Do you?"

"No."

"Because you don't want to try?"

"Because oil and vinegar don't mix."

She shifted in her seat to face him. "But we're not salad ingredients, Logan. We're human beings, capable of changing if we have the desire."

"By all means," he drawled, annoyed that out of the corner of his eye he continued to see too much of her tanned, smooth thighs, "tell me about what you desire."

Maybe the comment was provocative, but she'd started it. She was the one who'd phrased herself so suggestively.

"I didn't mean that in a sexual way."

"Of course not."

"I didn't! Why do you always have to assume that just because my mother was a—was who she was," she amended, her tone almost smoky, "that I'm the same way?"

He frowned at the incredible comparison. "I wasn't thinking of your mother at all."

"You weren't?"

"I was strictly referring to you and my brother."

"Oh."

It annoyed him to hear her sound as if she hadn't a clue as to what he was talking about. "The times I caught you two so close a crowbar couldn't have pried you apart."

She looked offended. "You never saw us necking or anything!"

True. But he wasn't about to cut her any slack for small favors. "What about the time I caught you two skinny-dipping together?"

"I couldn't very well have worn my shorts and shirt in, and I wasn't wearing any underwear beneath it. That had to be saved for school."

Logan thought he could have gone the rest of his life without having heard *that*. His mind, ever ready to taunt him, fantasized about what she might not be wearing under her jeans and top now, and he shifted, his body reacting traitorously.

"All right, what about the time I came in from work to find you two sprawled across his bed?"

"He was trying to help me with my algebra, and we were whispering so as not to disturb your mother."

"Yeah, that's why you looked so guilty when I opened the door."

"Well, you should have seen your face," Merri countered. "You looked angrier than a preacher reprimanding kids for whispering in church. Your expression is almost as threatening now, and there's just the two of us here."

If she reminded him that they were alone once more, he was going to get out and walk the rest of the way home. "And you need to ask if a truce is possible? Neither one of us can direct a statement at the other without attacking or being sarcastic."

"Why do you suppose we do that?"

Did she really have no clue? "Hasn't it crossed your mind that we just don't like each other?"

"No. I think there's a 'because' to everything, and I think you hate me because I took your brother away from you. You don't seem to realize that someone would have, eventually. At any rate, you two were the ones who were polar opposites."

It made sense, but Logan knew that wasn't *it*. At least not completely. He realized that now. Maybe he'd known back then, too; he just hadn't felt like admitting it to himself.

His real gripe was that she'd been drawn to Brett instead of him. As the thought settled in his mind, Logan felt a strange combination of pain and acceptance. It swept through him like a hot wind, and left him feeling some sense of resolution, and more than a little drained. Exhaling, he relaxed against the seat's headrest.

"You know I'm right, don't you?" Meredith asked, almost gently.

"If it's important for you to be right, believe what you want."

"Being right isn't the—" She made a sound of frustration. "All right. Tell me what you believe our problem is."

He debated the wisdom in putting his thoughts into words. Once they were out there, they had a tendency to haunt you forever.

After a few seconds, he turned his head to meet her somber, troubled gaze. Her closeness made his fingers itch to touch her. Simply looking at her made him ache with a new, and at the same time very old, longing. He suspected that if they actually did get beyond taking verbal swipes at each other, if they touched...kissed...they would probably spontaneously combust.

Never unhappier in his life, he surrendered to her will. "Chemistry."

For an instant he thought she was going to deny it—or, worse, make some sarcastic comment about him being the last man on earth she would be attracted to. He stiffened, trying to anticipate the pain denial and rejection would bring. Instead she, too, leaned back against the headrest, although the way she was sitting, it was her left temple that sought the comfort of leather.

"I was hoping I was wrong."

He wished her reaction didn't leave him with such a strong sense of relief. "Same here."

"Maybe we are wrong," she added hopefully. "After all, how can it be, when we're practically strangers?"

"We were veritable strangers back then, too."

"Yes, but what I mean is that maybe we're reacting to something that's not really there. Something like those false echoes on a weather radar screen, when it looks as if it's pouring all over, but the rain isn't reaching the ground?"

Logan's only response was to lift one eyebrow. It earned him a grimace from her.

"Well, it was worth a try." She crossed her arms beneath her breasts. "And for what it's worth, I'm sorry."

He grunted. "No more than me."

"What are we going to do about it?"

That was rich. After all those years of telling him to butt out of her life, she was asking for his advice? "The same thing we've been doing."

"You mean either fight or try to avoid each other? That's terrible! And it's not fair to your mother or Danny."

It was difficult to think about fairness, when he could barely keep his gaze from drifting downward. Her position was stretching her top across her breasts, and he could see that once again she wasn't wearing a bra. Despite the increasing darkness, the truck's dashboard lights gave off enough of a glow. There was no missing the twin peaks jutting against the knit jersey.

For his own peace of mind, he swung his gaze to the front again, and attempted an indifferent shrug. "You could always leave."

She didn't reply. For countless seconds he sat there, listening to the truck idling, the air conditioner working overtime, and his conscience calling him several choice names, none of which used more than seven letters.

"You must despise me more than I'd imagined," she said at last.

She'd spoken so quietly, he'd almost missed the observation. "*Despise* is getting a bit dramatic, but we've both worked too hard not to have had some success at disliking each other." However, dislike wasn't what he was feeling right now. He was realizing that he didn't want to hurt her. He just wanted her to understand. He wanted his sanity back.

"The past is over, Meredith. If we could leave it there, that would be enough for me. But I'm not sure it's going to be possible if you stay on here."

"Your mother wants us, Logan. She's lonely. What's more, Danny needs the connection. The poor guy's been dragged over so much territory in his young life, he's sadly lacking in a sense of roots and tradition. I can see it's affected him, hurt his confidence and self-esteem. You add that to his sensitivity over his small size, and you have a kid who's had a difficult time making friends.''

Hell, Logan thought, feeling his world closing in on him. That wasn't his problem. He didn't want to feel sorry for any of them. Why was it that, as usual, *he* was the only one who was supposed to do any adjusting or sacrificing?

''Please?''

The touch of her hand on his forearm jarred him out of his brooding. He'd removed his jacket and rolled up his sleeves, and as he looked down at her small hand against his bronzed flesh, he found himself imagining moving it elsewhere. His body stirred to life as awareness grew into hunger. When he lifted his gaze to Meredith's again, her lips parted on a silent gasp at what obviously showed on his face.

He wanted to take her mouth with his, to finally learn what she tasted like, to discover the sounds she made when passion won control over reason. But most of all—

''Logan...I— You can't. I still feel like Brett's wife.''

Without another word, he removed her hand from his arm and sat forward. Putting the truck into gear, he drove the rest of the way to the house.

As soon as he parked beside his mother's station wagon, he grabbed his jacket from the hook behind him and climbed out. He didn't bother looking back to see if Meredith followed until he reached the kitchen door. She hadn't. She'd just gotten out, and she simply stood by the truck, watching him with the same bruised, wary look he remembered from the old days when they'd had a head-on collision of temperaments.

He didn't, couldn't, let it get to him.

"One more thing," he added tersely. "In the future, keep your hands to yourself. Unless you're ready for the consequences."

Three

Three

―――

As May inched lazily into June, Logan discovered how well Meredith could follow directives. She not only avoided any physical contact with him, she managed to all but stay out of sight.

He had to give her points for effort, he thought on the first Friday of the month, as he pulled into the driveway and saw her spot his truck and retreat into the house. He had a feeling there'd been a time when she wouldn't have resisted calling his bluff, for the sheer enjoyment of driving him nuts. But these days, except for rare instances when he got home from work early enough to eat dinner with the three of them, he hardly knew she was in the house. Although an early riser herself, she would linger in her room until he left in the morning, and at night she always made an excuse for escaping by murmuring about wanting to do some reading or getting some letters written.

He was grateful for the respite, but at the same time didn't expect it to last. Why forget the old saying about a leopard's inability to change its spots? he reminded himself as he once again parked beside his mother's station wagon. Meredith could no more change who she was at her core than he could. That meant the day had to come when their temperaments would clash again. It was only a question of when.

As he exited the vehicle, he paused to take his first real breath of the sultry late-spring day he'd almost missed, and experienced a momentary sweet pleasure. For all his brooding, things could be worse. They had been worse. When he returned from the war, hadn't he had to relearn to accept beauty, time…peace? Back then, he'd felt guilty for having survived. Undeserving. He just needed to keep reminding himself that this strange arrangement they were in could be adjusted to, as well. They only needed to take each day as it came.

About to head inside, he saw Sherman waving to him from the side of the barn. Before he could call to him, the old man touched a finger to his lips and motioned him over.

"What's up?" he asked, joining him in the lengthening shadows.

The farmer's face, like a mask made of ancient, mahogany-colored leather, crinkled into a thousand lines as he eased back his worn straw hat to scratch at his short-cropped white hair. "Don't wanna upset the boy any mo' than he already is."

"Daniel? What's wrong with him?"

"Can't figure it. 'Bout an hour ago, he come home from bein' out yonder somewheres and went straight fo' the barn. Got hisself a fat lip and bloody nose, tell you that much. Reckon his mama thinks he was with friends, an' he don't want her t' see different. But he wouldn' tell me. Thought mebbe you'd have better luck."

"Me?" The mere idea had Logan wanting to head back to his truck and head for the hills. "I don't know anything about dealing with kids, Sherman."

"You was a boy. You knows 'bout gettin' into fights."

He couldn't argue with that. He'd had to handle his share, thanks to the skirmishes Brett had run away from. Was the kid like his old man? That was just what he needed.

"Hell. All right. I'll see what I can do," he said to the old-timer. "Thanks for telling me."

"Aw, don' be lookin' like that. He's a nice kid. Comes out t' watch me sometimes. Helps Miz Faith 'round the yard, too. Likes the earth, I can see that. Could be you got some-body t' take my place after I pass on."

For once, Logan's crooked smile came easily. "You aren't allowed to go anywhere, Sherman. You and that cantan-kerous tractor you won't let me replace will be an institu-tion around here until the sun stops rising."

Chuckling gleefully, Sherman waved a goodbye and headed off toward his cottage on the other side of the driveway. A nice man, Logan thought for hardly the first time, but too darned generous in judging people. Sher-man's own marriage had failed way back when Logan was knee-high to a crawdad. He'd fallen for a lusty, roving-eyed woman called Belle, who—only months after the wed-ding—had decided she wanted more than being the wife of a sharecropper, and had taken Sherman's life savings and run off, never to be seen again. It hadn't soured the man's view of life one iota.

Thinking about that, Logan flipped his jacket over his shoulder and went in the opposite direction. When he stepped past the opened doors of the barn, it was dark and cool inside, but there was enough light for him to quickly locate the boy, sitting with his back to a chest-high pallet of sacked fertilizer. The instant Daniel realized Logan had spotted him, he turned his head away.

"You okay?" Logan asked, deciding it would be better not to pretend he didn't know something was wrong.

"I guess."

"Want me to take a look?"

"Nah. I'll live. I just don't want to show my mom. She's going to bust a seam when she sees what a mess I am."

Logan knew the boy had begun summer school recently, to catch up on what he'd missed due to his father's illness and the move down here. He'd also heard enough in the house to determine that Daniel was one of the smaller kids in the sophomore class, and sensitive about the subject. Sensitive to the point where he wouldn't fear picking a fight after school? Logan needed to find out.

"What's the other guy look like?"

"Ready for a cover-model shoot. I never got near enough to mark him."

"What started it all?"

The boy ducked his head lower. "Pick something. I'm the new kid, shorter than the other guys, and... and they all know about my dad."

Logan had guessed it might be something like that. He doubted Meredith and Brett had dwelled much on what Brett's decisions would mean to Daniel once he returned to the States.

Logan hunkered down before him, eyed the kid's bruised knuckles before inspecting his injured face. "Well, at least you tried to fight back."

"A lot of good it did me. I got this going straight into that hickory tree down by the pond." He held up his hand for a better view.

"Then you're lucky you didn't break it. How big was the other guy?"

"A head taller than me, but what difference does it make? He has enough friends to back him up, no matter what. And I'll tell you something else, I don't care if I do get left back, I'm not going back to tomorrow's algebra class. He'll cremate me."

Logan hadn't heard that expression since he'd been a student. "You'll need algebra if you want to get into college."

"So I won't go. My dad didn't."

Logan wasn't about to drive into that pothole. He decided that he would have better luck trying a different tactic with the boy.

"Do you want to learn how to keep that bully from getting at you again?"

Despite a moment's flicker of interest, his nephew ducked his head again and offered an indifferent shrug. "Why bother? I'm no boxer."

"I don't mean boxing. I'm talking about defending yourself."

The curiosity returned, intensified. "You mean like karate stuff?"

"Just some basic moves we learned in the service. Enough to make bullies like the guy who got the best of you today realize you're not a pushover."

"That would be great." The teen scrambled to his feet. "Can we start now?"

Logan wanted to suggest that tomorrow would be soon enough, but one look at the poor kid's face, and the blood on his shirt, and he felt his resistance fracture. "All right." He sought a place to hook his jacket and settled on a nail. "Okay, take a swing at me."

"You're kidding."

"Go ahead. Try it."

Fear crept into the boy's eyes. "Is this going to hurt? I mean, I'm game, but..."

As the youngster swallowed, Logan shook his head. He definitely had his work cut out for him. Somehow he had to teach his nephew that you couldn't let anyone know you were scared, not at his age or later in life. But at least he had to give the kid credit for having the courage to try.

"It won't hurt. Just take a swing...and pay attention."

It took the teen several seconds more before he gained the courage to aim a blow at Logan's jaw. Before the fist came anywhere near him, however, Logan thrust out his left arm and deflected it.

"Hey!" Danny stared, astonished. "How'd you do that?"

"Try using your forearm and momentum to thwart my move. Now try it again."

Danny tried three more times, a fourth, and each time Logan deflected the swings. The sad thing was, as increasingly bold as his nephew grew, Logan barely felt any pain from the contact at all. The kid needed all the help someone could give him.

"Now you give it a shot," he told him.

The first time, he held back, to let Daniel get a feel for the moves and angles. Then, with each progressive swing, he felt the boy's confidence grow.

"Okay," he said after the tenth swing. "Now I'm going to come at you at normal speed. Pretend this is the real thing."

He saw the trepidation return to the boy's eyes. But no sooner did he position himself than he felt something swat him hard in the middle of his back.

"What the—?" He swung around, barely in time to dodge another slap from the broom Meredith was aiming at him.

"Get away from my boy, Logan Powers!" Then Meredith saw her son's face. "My God, Danny! What on earth—How *dare* you beat my child, you...you..."

Logan grabbed hold of the broom to slow her down. "Easy, Meredith. Think it out, and you'll know you have it all wrong."

"Yeah, Mom. Calm down. A guy from school did this," Danny added, his voice breaking under the urgency of the moment. "Logan's only trying to teach me to defend myself."

Her expression reflected surprise and a touch of embarrassment before she stiffened again. "I thought we'd discussed the subject of fighting, Danny."

Before he could respond, Logan said, "Boys can't avoid a few skirmishes while growing up. He tried, and look what happened."

"Excuse me, but I was talking to my son." Meredith's icy disdain melted only when she turned to her boy. "Go on inside and get cleaned up. We'll talk later, after I clear up a few things with your uncle."

"Aw, Mom...I want to learn more."

"Do what your mother says, Dan. We can continue this tomorrow," Logan told him with a nod of reassurance.

Danny did leave, but the instant he was out of sight, Meredith jerked at the broom, nearly knocking Logan off-balance. "You will *not* continue anything of the kind!"

"He needs help."

"Then I'll help him use his brains instead of brawn! It's difficult enough to know he has to grow up in a violent world. Do you think a few macho moves will change anything?"

"Yes, if you'll quit babying him long enough to give him a chance to learn them."

This time she aimed the broom for his head. Logan ducked, then jerked the thing out of her grasp. After he tossed it behind him, he grabbed her and hauled her close, using his body to keep her still.

"Don't ever try that again," he told her, seething, an inch away from yielding to some unspeakable violence.

"I'll do more than try," she vowed, breathless.

Logan shook his head. "You know, if your boy had an ounce of your fire, he wouldn't have any problems. So why are you trying to turn him into another Brett?"

"I'm not trying anything of the kind. I've worked hard to instill the idea in Danny that first and foremost he's unique unto himself. There's nothing that gets me steamed faster than someone saying, 'Oh, you're just like this person or that person.'"

"Okay," Logan said, hearing an edge in her voice that he knew better than to provoke. "Consider the lesson learned."

"Don't patronize me. And let me tell you something else. Despite what you think of his father, there are people who will remember Brett as a sensitive and talented man!"

When he wasn't lazy, conniving, and a coward, Logan thought, narrowing his eyes because she sounded a bit too desperate.

"He cared about his art and bringing something beautiful to the world. Anything he created during his short life was a masterpiece compared to the cruelty that *you* manifested!"

Now she'd gone too far. Logan couldn't listen to another word. Having Meredith this close was tough enough on his nerves. Hearing her accusations that he was equivalent to some monster was too much. Deciding there was only one quick way to silence her, he crushed his mouth to hers.

Her shock rippled through him, followed by the heat of her embarrassment as she grew increasingly sensitive to their intimate stance. Good, he thought, aware of every inch of her slim, small body; but he wondered why it took this blatant contact, why it had to be *her* body for his to grow this hard, this fast. He'd never felt this incredibly alive before—all while still spitting mad.

She began fighting him, so he caught her hands, pressed his entire body into hers, and deepened the kiss. While he couldn't bring himself to be gentle, he soon discovered he couldn't be cruel, either. All he knew was the most amazing need to have more of her. And more. It blinded him to every other emotion, until there was only *her*.

Despite her furious twists and thrusts to free herself, he prolonged the kiss, which inflamed her further. As bold as it was unapologetic, his stroking became an unmistakable mating that perpetuated the ache in his groin. Soon he was nudging her backward until, with a thud, she came up hard against the supply room wall. Then, stooping slightly, he nestled his throbbing flesh in the apex of her thighs.

He swallowed her startled gasp, and fed her his moan of pleasure. Nothing could have felt more perfect, except maybe having her on a bed, with both of them naked. He lifted his head to see if he would find the same thoughts reflected in her eyes, and when he did, it was all he could do not to draw her down onto the cool cement floor with him.

Releasing her hands, he shifted his to her breasts, stroking his thumbs across her taut nipples. "I want you," he whispered. His voice had never been more gravelly. "I want you so badly, I can barely stand it."

"We can't."

"Hell, don't I know it? But it doesn't change the truth."

"Please don't do that anymore."

"What? This?" He purposely grazed his thumbs across her nipples again, loving the choked moan of sweet torture he won from her. "I remember what color you are here. A dusky rose. I've dreamed about it. About putting my mouth on you."

"Logan, this is insane. Your mother has dinner almost ready. If we don't get inside, she's going to come looking for us."

Ignoring her, he repeated the caress. "Something's going to come of this."

"No."

"It has to. We can't go on... and the feeling's getting stronger."

She swallowed and stared up at him with eyes at once vulnerable and wounded. "Is this just another attempt to make me... make us leave?"

He thought about that, wanting to be sure that when he answered it wouldn't be anything less than the truth. "No. But I do have to warn you that if you stay, I'm coming after you."

"Wh-what do you mean?"

"You know."

Staring as if he'd just announced he'd arrived from some other planet, Meredith shook her head once and scrambled away from him. Backing toward the exit, she warned him, "I'm going inside now."

"Fine. I'll be in shortly."

"And we're going to forget this happened."

"You can try."

"Logan." She pressed her hands to her temples. "Why are you doing this?"

He simply shook his head. "Who's doing what to whom... Merri?"

* * *

Merri had to struggle not to run back to the house. The only thing that allowed her to stay her panic was the possibility that Faith might be looking out the window and see her. The thought spawned a new rush of self-consciousness, and she lifted a hand to her lips. They stung from Logan's kisses, his whiskers. Would Faith be able to tell? Guilt became a powerful enemy, and she began thinking of excuses to keep out of the kitchen—or at least to delay sitting down to dinner for a few minutes.

Blast Logan for this. It had been bad enough to see him teaching Danny things she didn't want her son to have to know about, but now this? It couldn't be happening.

"Is everything all right?" Faith called, the instant Merri opened the back door.

She knew there was no way she could answer that. "Did Danny go upstairs?" she called back, hoping Faith would guess she hadn't heard her.

"Like a hummingbird negotiating the pillars and hanging baskets on our front porch at seventy miles per hour. I didn't see him, because I was on the phone. As soon as I get these rolls out of the—"

Merri peeked around the doorway, saw Faith leaning into the stove, and saw her chance. She dashed across the kitchen and hesitated at the stairs to call, "Okay. Be right with you!" Then she hurried upstairs.

The main bathroom door across from Danny's bedroom was shut. Merri decided he had to be in there. It was just as well. She figured that at the moment she didn't want him to see her any more than he wanted her to see him.

She passed her room and Logan's and went to the smaller bathroom in the master bedroom. Upon their return to Rachel, Faith had made it clear that she was welcome to use it anytime.

Well, she needed the vanity mirror. Now.

"Oh, *no...*" she wailed softly the instant she saw her reflection.

The good news was that, despite her sensitive skin, there weren't any whisker burns. But her eyes had never sparkled so, her cheeks had never burned this fever red. As for her lips... What had she said to Logan about parking or necking? Dear heaven, that was exactly what she looked as if she'd been doing.

Staring, she used her fingertips to trace the path of his kisses over her lips. It was a mistake. Once again she tasted him, relived his relentless exploration, the way his heat had burned into her breasts, her womb, and lower. As her legs began to tremble again, she gripped the counter.

"I want you."

She wanted him, too. That was the worst of it. No, the worst of it was finally accepting that the feelings had always been there, like he'd said, only she'd been too young, too dumb, to face them.

Stifling a sob of anguish and shame, she wrenched on the cold-water tap and bent low to splash the refreshing liquid over her face, desperate to wash away the hot images searing her mind. It seemed to take forever for her cheeks and lips to stop burning. In the process, she soaked the hair framing her face, but she'd ceased caring. She could just think up another excuse to cover up the truth, couldn't she? Another lie. She'd become a master at lying.

Finally she turned off the tap and dried off. Yes, she looked better. Normal in a strangely remote kind of way, but less... kissed. That was all that mattered.

"Mom?"

The sound of her name gave Merri a jolt. "In here, honey. I'm coming."

Quickly hanging up the towel, she fingered her hair into some order and exited the bathroom. Danny stood just outside the master bedroom, hands shoved in his pockets, a clean T-shirt replacing the bloodied one. He, too, had washed, and his hair was damp and freshly combed. But it was his swollen lip and bruised cheekbone that drew most of her attention.

She ached to sweep him into her arms and rock him as she had when he was a baby. Naturally, those days were over. If she hadn't realized it yet, his cautionary step backward brought the truth home with the impact of a blow to her heart. Her little boy was becoming a man, and wanted to be treated like one. And here she'd been acting with less maturity than he.

Don't think about you. Focus on his needs.

"Hi, Tiger. Feel better?"

"I'll live. I thought I heard the water running in here, and I wanted to make sure you and Uncle Logan hadn't killed each other."

Merri ducked her head to avoid too close an inspection. "Not quite. I'm sorry I jumped to conclusions out there."

"I guess you can't help being a mother."

"Thanks so much."

"You know what I mean."

"Unfortunately. Will you tell me how long you've been having trouble in school? I mean this school."

"What difference does it make? You know it's the same thing no matter where we go. It just gets tougher the older I get. I guess the guys have more to prove, because the cliques are more established or something. I don't know."

"How do I help you?" she asked. She'd never felt more useless. Sure, she'd known about the kids teasing him about being smaller and rather small-boned, and that his quiet personality made making new friends difficult for him. But she'd never heard this pain in his voice before.

"Hey, I'll survive."

Dear heaven, did that sound uncomfortably familiar! "I don't want you simply to survive!" she cried softly, wrapping her arms around her middle. "I told you that I was a misfit in school. Those were the most horrible years of my life. I never wanted you to have to endure that, and I thought you were doing better than I did."

"You were supposed to think that. It was the least I could do while you were working so hard to make ends meet, when Dad was having a tough time with his work. Seeing you always trying to be cheerful when sometimes you looked ready to drop made me feel ashamed about feeling sorry for myself."

He'd seen that, too? "I *was* cheerful," she insisted, needing him to understand that. "You were my family, and I loved to do things for you guys."

"Like you had a big choice," Danny replied with a grimace. "I know everybody liked Dad, but his stuff didn't bring in much."

Dazed, Merri touched her forehead. "Whoa! You're blowing this old lady's mind."

"Come on...cut it out. You have more energy than most of the girls in my school."

"The flattery's falling on deaf ears, kiddo, because I'm ticked that I let myself believe you hadn't noticed all that. And I knew better! When I was your age, I noticed *everything*." She stared at him as if seeing him for the first time. "I'm sorry. I see that I must have been trying to keep you from growing up, or at least growing up too fast, so I tried to hide life from you. That was wrong."

"You were trying to protect me because you knew Dad couldn't."

Merri winced at the harsh truth. "Oh, Danny. He did love you, though. You know that, don't you? Maybe he wasn't the type to play baseball with you, or take you camping, like other boys' fathers, and he certainly didn't know anything about self-defense, but . . . you were a miracle to him."

"I know." Although he glanced away, a faint, sheepish smile crossed his lips. "It's not every guy whose father read him *Ivanhoe* and *Don Quixote* before *Peter Pan*."

Brett had had more in common with Peter Pan, Merri thought with another twinge of sadness and guilt. He'd been the dreamer, the boy who didn't want to face reality and focused on a more idealistic world instead.

But it had worked out. She hadn't minded taking on the breadwinner's role in the family. Her own background had all but groomed her for it, creating in her a fierce craving for a family she could care for and nourish the way she hadn't been loved herself. But she was beginning to realize that such logic hadn't been right, or fair to Danny.

"I guess what I'm really here to say to you is that I'm realizing I'm not Dad, Mom. But I'm not you, either," Danny continued, his expression once again somber. "I'm not really sure where that leaves me, or who I'm gonna end up being as an adult, but I do know I want to learn how to fight back if I have to. Uncle Logan can teach me stuff like that, Mom. Most important, I want him to."

Merri felt torn in two. On the one hand, she knew she would be letting her son down if she asked him not to protect himself from bullies. Hadn't she been willing to whip the tar out of Logan when she thought he might be provoking her boy? But, on the other hand, she truly believed that violence resolved nothing, just bred more violence. How did she help her son determine his own answers without abandoning her own convictions?

"It's not as if I'm going to forget all that you and Dad have tried to teach me," he insisted, as if she'd spoken out loud.

And she'd been worrying about him? Maybe she should be asking him for advice. Impressed, and ever so proud, she reached out to lightly touch his bruised cheek. "How'd you get so smart, mister?"

"Guess I had some good teachers." With a glance over his shoulder, he added, "You ready to go downstairs before Gran threatens to send up a search party?"

Not really. But she knew better than to say so. "Lead the way."

Arm in arm, they walked down the hall. As they approached the top of the stairs, Danny cast her a worried glance. "What about Uncle Logan? Did you two get things straightened out?"

Talk about understatements. Merri would have laughed, if her insides didn't feel like an undercooked omelet. "Sweetheart, I'm not sure your uncle and I will get to the point where we don't register on the Richter scale whenever we come face-to-face. But you might say we have an uneasy cease-fire, while we try to come to terms with some things." That was stretching the truth big-time, but under no circumstances would she upset him again today.

"I guess that's better than anticipating World War III over meat loaf."

His spirits clearly buoyed somewhat by their talk and Logan's offer to help him, Danny was surprisingly upbeat and talkative throughout dinner. Merri continued to watch him for any sign that his attitude was just a brave front, but had to admit she was grateful that he seemed sincere. She certainly didn't feel like conversing.

Faith, too, seemed happier than she'd been since their arrival. Of course, Merri amended wryly, she'd caught a glimpse of her with Stan Shirley earlier in the afternoon, and she had a feeling that might have been him on the phone a few minutes ago.

"You'll have to ask your mother about that."

Logan's deep, cautious tone immediately told Merri that she'd missed something important. Avoiding his gaze, she looked at her son. "Excuse me. Ask me what?"

"Dan voiced an interest in helping Sherman and maybe learning more about farming," Logan replied, despite her dismissal. "I warned him that it was a tough life, but if he was serious, Sherman could teach him quite a bit to catch him up with what the kids in school agricultural classes had been learning. Even so, if he was going to pursue the matter, he needed to clear it with you."

Farming? Danny hadn't said anything about farming upstairs, and it was a polar opposite to his interest in self-defense instruction. She wouldn't stand in her son's way, no matter what direction he chose for his life, but she had to admit he certainly was keeping her guessing what that might eventually be.

"Well . . ." She glanced at Faith for guidance. No way would she look at Logan. As it was, she didn't know what he was up to, either. Surely he wouldn't use Danny to fulfill his threat to her?

"Logan's right," the older woman offered gently. "Few people have Sherman's understanding of the land, and he possesses a wonderful talent for sharing that knowledge. What your generation would have called a 'laid-back' quality, I suppose."

"And look at it this way, Mom," Danny interjected. "If I turn out to be any good at it, you wouldn't have to worry about putting me through college."

"Oh, now, wait a minute," Merri replied, not liking the sound of that at all.

"May I respond to that?" Faith waited for Merri to nod. Turning to her grandson, she continued, "Your uncle has no interest in the farm, nor does he need the money it would bring by selling it. If you decide farming is the right vocation for you, college would still be a must. You see, technology has become a necessity. But you would be that much farther ahead with your knowledge of the old ways and the new. What's more, I'd be proud to pay for your college tuition."

Merri couldn't believe what she was hearing. Faith's invitation to stay on had meant the world to her. Even so, Merri had begun studying the want ads, unwilling to keep taking from Faith without giving back. This latest gesture went beyond generosity.

She stared at Faith, unable to think of anything to say. Danny seemed overcome, too, and barely managed an awed "Wow."

Although the older woman reached over to pat Danny's hand, she focused on Merri. "Why the shock, dear? You're family. Who else should I spoil?"

Danny gave a hoot of delight and sprang from his chair to hug his grandmother. Merri watched in a daze, but, aware that if anyone could snap her back to reality it was Logan, she cast him a cautious look. It turned out to be the worst thing she could have done.

He was already watching her, and his gaze reflected more than a hint of mockery, but also she saw a flicker of the emotions he'd exposed to her in the barn. It was as if he were challenging her by saying, "Now what are you going to do?" and she was ashamed when, despite a spasm of fear, her body reignited with yearning and heat.

In near desperation, she refocused on the laughing duo. "I'm glad he can think of something to say, Faith. I'm afraid I just don't have the words."

Later, she tried to concentrate on Danny's happiness to ease the growing anxiety that kept her from falling asleep. She'd never seen him so excited before. But that euphoria was going to prove her downfall, because now she knew there was no way she could take Danny from here without breaking his spirit. And *that* meant dealing with Logan and his promise.

Maybe it had all been a bluff, she thought as she tossed in her bed for the umpteenth time. Surely he wouldn't follow through with it? In his mother's house?

But he'd managed to do quite a bit in the barn, hadn't he?

"I'm coming after you."

"Oh, God," she moaned into her pillow, "I don't want this."

However, long into the night she kept reliving those torrid kisses, the feel of his hands on her body, the way she'd responded. He'd made a liar out of her. She did want it, want him.

She would just have to fight the weakness. Danny's future lay in her hands. She had to stay out of Logan's grasp.

Four

"I'll drive you."

Merri went still, hoping she hadn't heard Logan correctly. How could this be happening to her, she wondered, when the whole point in taking this job after weeks of searching the papers was to spend *less* time with him, not *more?*

"Why, that's a wonderful idea, dear," Faith said, once again beaming across the dinner table at her son and then back to Merri. "He can bring you to work—after all, the café is right on his way to his office—and I'll pick you up on my way from collecting Danny at summer school. Of course, I wish you'd believed me when I told you that it's not necessary for you to get a job."

"Could be Meredith's bored with the quiet life and needs some action," Logan suggested, before Merri could reiterate her position on the matter.

She ignored him. "I need to feel as if I'm contributing to the family," she told Faith. "I know waitressing the breakfast and lunch shifts at Angel's Café isn't Logan's idea of a real job—"

"I didn't say anything of the kind," he said mildly as he reached for his favorite salad dressing.

She barely refrained from kicking his shin under the table. "The point is, it's honest work."

"Then it's perfect for an honest woman, isn't it?"

Unable to ignore the innuendo, Merri shot him a look that spoke volumes. He smiled back, but what she noted was that the smile didn't quite reach his dark eyes.

"Logan, do behave," his mother pleaded, sounding anything but pleased herself.

Wide-eyed, he sat back in his chair. "I thought I was. I'm offering to drive her, aren't I?"

Merri chose to remain silent in response to that, as well. She knew if she said anything else, someone would end up upset enough not to finish dinner—and that someone would be her. Besides not wanting to upset Danny, she didn't want Faith to know that although it was now mid-July, and their lives had settled into a relatively comfortable pattern, there was still as much friction between her and Logan as there had been two months ago. Maybe more.

She turned her attention to her son. "You're okay with this, aren't you? I mean, you're in classes during that time, anyway."

"Sure, Mom. I think Gran's going to be the one who'll be most affected by this. She's gotten used to having you around."

"Absolutely." Faith passed Merri the basket of sliced bread. "On the other hand, I understand and respect your decision, dear. It's time you got out and saw more people, too. Life must go on."

Realizing what she meant, Merri adamantly shook her head. "I'm not interested in anything like that. What I'm concerned about is that once the regular school year starts next month, Danny's going to need new clothes. But I have to add, Faith, my presence around here day in and day out is keeping *you* from doing all you might like."

Her mother-in-law looked sincerely shocked. "How on earth did you come to that— You're not keeping me from anything, Merri. I've loved every minute we've spent together. It's you I'm worrying about."

"Really, I'm fine."

"Are you? Let me say something, dear. Even an old country girl like me knows that you need more human contact than you get around here."

Merri gestured, at a loss over her mother-in-law's opinion of herself. "Faith, we haven't seen each other in years. I was married to your youngest son. What you might think of as boring for me, I've seen as us catching up on each other's lives. What's so terrible about that?"

"You're sweet—and when you put it that way, I'm even flattered. But my instincts tell me to encourage you to reach out to new opportunities, and people."

She didn't like what that suggested at all. She had enough problems with *people* as it was. "You know, on second thought there's still time before I really have to worry about shopping for school things. I could—"

"No, I've been selfish long enough. You take that job and get yourself some spending money so you can splurge on yourself once in a while."

"Does this mean I'll get to have lunch at Angel's instead of eating the crummy cafeteria food?" Danny asked, the most enthusiastic one of all.

Merri managed to smile at that. "Forget it. Angel's idea of cooking healthy is adding a radish garnish to his deep-fried entrées."

"Why do I get the feeling poor Angel's due for an unwelcome lecture or two from the new help?"

Logan's droll observation broke a silence that had led Merri to believe he'd tired of needling her. "It was Angel who wanted me to start working today." She wasn't about to let him undermine her ability. "He was fascinated that I was single-handedly managing a small grill in Calgary six days a week for fourteen hours a day."

"My, my... What job *haven't* you held since your days at old man Monroe's garage?"

She gave him a killer smile. "When you haven't had the opportunities some people have, you learn to be grateful for what comes your way."

"No doubt. But what was the poet laureate doing while you were flipping flapjacks?"

Merri's smile froze. She didn't dare look at Danny, for fear he would see her embarrassment and hurt, or at Faith, because it would only lead to questions she didn't want to answer. In the end, she didn't have to. Faith took control of the conversation.

"I think it's wonderful that you became something of a jack-of-all-trades," she said, before turning to her oldest son. "And do you know why? If it wasn't for Merri hearing the car making a strange noise the other day—which, I might add, I completely missed—I would have driven off, and the fan belt would have broken midway between here and town, leaving me stranded in one-hundred-degree heat. Instead, she located an extra in the barn that I would never have thought to look for, and saved me time and untold aggravation. Brett was a lucky man to have a wife so talented in her own right."

"Thank you, Mother," Logan drawled, saluting her with his fork. "Rest assured, I've been put properly in my place." He glanced back at Merri, his expression turning enigmatic. "As I said, I'll drive you. Be down here at six tomorrow."

Merri was on time the next morning, and each morning after that. For ten days they made the drive without saying a word to each other. She couldn't say she was sorry.

Despite the cold shoulder from Logan, Merri soon realized she'd done the right thing in taking the job at Angel's. The café's burly, rough-voiced proprietor had a heart as pure as his nickname suggested, and she found the other waitresses a friendly bunch, too. In fact, except for the clientele, who were mostly downtown businesspeople on the run, the place wasn't all that different from where she'd worked in Canada. Well, with one exception—the tips she earned seemed to get better with every day.

By the beginning of her third week there, Merri had made enough money to make a good start on replenishing Danny's wardrobe, and to buy herself two more uniforms. The little black dresses were not unlike those nurses wore in white. Most of the other waitresses—regardless of size—tended to wear theirs flirtatiously short. Merri knew she had the figure to wear the miniskirt length, but although the girls encouraged her to "go for it," she hemmed hers to remain slightly longer. They were still short, though, and got shorter, particularly when she had to climb into Logan's pickup truck. She wished she had anticipated that before it was too late.

"Why the devil don't you wear something at a respectable length? Then you wouldn't have that problem," he muttered the next morning, as she once again tugged the skirt down after climbing into his vehicle.

"It *is* at a respectable length. It's the height of this truck that's the problem," she snapped back at him. "Good grief, a woman would have to wear coveralls not to embarrass herself getting into this thing."

"Which is about the last thing we'll see you wearing again, isn't it? No juicy tips from ogling customers that way."

Securing her seat belt, Merri blew her bangs out of her eyes and glared at him as he cranked the engine and tore down the driveway. "To what do I owe the honor of your commentary, anyway? I thought we'd developed a very satisfying routine of silence."

"That little display of female helplessness just now demanded something."

"Female— I definitely like the cold-shoulder treatment better. Feel free to resume the status quo any time you're ready." Precarious though it was at this speed, she released her seat belt to lean forward and tie the shoelace on one of her tennis shoes, which she'd inadvertently stepped on.

"Will you get that belt buckled?"

"I will. Could I finish with this first, please?"

"Fine. If I get a ticket, you'll pay it."

"Logan, in the past three weeks we haven't seen another human being on this farm-to-market road. The jackrabbits are barely awake! So what is your problem?"

"You."

"Well, if you paid as much attention to your driving as you do to me and my clothes, you'd get me out of this truck sooner."

They'd reached the first stop sign down the road. Instead of continuing on through, Logan abruptly shifted into park and lunged across the bench seat at her. He shot his hand around to her nape and brought her nose to nose with him.

"That's it. No more, do you hear me?"

"I won't be bullied, Logan," Merri managed, although her heart had begun to pound in her ears.

"And I won't be told how to drive. I haven't been issued a ticket in twenty years, and I don't need any advice from you."

"Well, I have a boss who tells me what to wear. I don't need any hassle from *you*."

"You're a Powers, and I have to do business around here. If you compromise yourself, it reflects on my reputation."

"Are you serious?" She shoved against his chest, though it proved about as effective as trying to budge one of Faith's giant oaks or magnolias. "You self-centered, sanctimonious...snob! Let me out of this thing. I'd rather walk and risk being fired for being late than ride another inch in your company."

But the harder she struggled to free herself, the tighter Logan held her. Suddenly she heard a telling snapping sound, and felt the cool breeze from the air-conditioning on a part of her anatomy that was previously covered.

"Oh, damn...now look what you've done."

Logan leaned back, apparently also aware of what had happened. Merri glanced down to confirm that the top button of her uniform had popped off, and swore under her breath.

"Where'd it go?"

"Let me turn the interior light on."

"No!" There was already enough daylight for him to see that she was wearing her one pretty bra, which made her look almost voluptuous. Though she'd originally purchased it, years ago, to wear for special occasions with Brett, she wore it nowadays because it was the only one she had that was black, like her uniforms. "Just get out of my way. I'll find it."

Merri unsnapped her seat belt and reached for the dark object she spotted on the floorboard. But Logan spotted it at the same moment. They bumped hands and sent the button flying over to his side of the truck.

"Stay still, I'll—"

"Will you let me?"

"You're going to knock the gearshift into drive and kill us both."

"Get your hand out of there!"

They both reacted as if they'd touched fire, and sprang into an upright position. Looking more disturbed than angry, Logan glanced down into the wide V of Merri's neckline just as she tried to tug it together.

"That was an accident."

"I'm not interested in excuses or apologies."

"If I'd wanted to touch you, I wouldn't have groped like a boy on his first date."

"Could I have my property back, please?"

He handed the button to her. "Do you have a needle and thread in your purse, or at least a safety pin?"

"Yes."

"Good." His voice had grown softer, deeper. "I don't want to think about other men seeing you the way I have."

Merri felt her breath rush from her lungs, felt an unwelcome tingling race through her blood. "Logan—" she swallowed "—we're in the middle of an intersection." When that didn't work, she continued, "We both have to get to work."

Instead of replying, he reached over to feel the pulse at her throat. "You can try to pretend that being this close doesn't affect you as much as it does me, but your body will never let you get away with it."

Before she could respond, he slipped his hand into her gaping uniform, and then her bra. Shocked at feeling him cupping her, she had no time to stop him when he quickly bent and replaced his hand with his mouth.

Merri cried out in surprise, as much as at the incredible, piercing pleasure that shot through her. It was sheer reflex that had her grasping his upper arms, but as he drew her deeper into his mouth, she found herself pulling him closer, instead of pushing him away. It was madness. It was the most erotic thing that had ever happened to her. Suddenly she didn't care if cars appeared on every side of them. There was only... this.

As quickly as he'd begun, Logan drew away and re- turned to his side of the truck. If appearance was anything to go by, he was feeling as much frustration as her, but af- ter doing little more than combing his hands through his hair, he shifted again and continued forward.

Had she just imagined this?

"We're getting close to town," he warned quietly.

It was enough to make her remember her appearance. As she wriggled and shifted to adjust her clothing, she also felt her indignation finally return with blissful speed. "You had no right to do that."

"Maybe. But I had no more choice about doing it than you had about responding to me."

She despised him more than ever at that moment. Not for his audacity, but for being right. "You're still intent on making me leave. Leave the only home I've really had."

"No. I'm trying to buy time. Hoping that if I appease at least a little of the hunger gnawing at me, something will happen to stop the inevitable."

She wanted to tell him that he was mad, to remind him that they had nothing in common to make them even think of a relationship, that she could never forgive him for how cruel he had been to Brett, how brutal he continued to be to his memory.

But before she could begin gathering her thoughts, he'd pulled up before the café. She had yet to say one word.

Coward.

"Just go, Meredith. There's nothing to say."

No, she thought as she climbed out, there wasn't. But there had to be something she could do. She had to make it clear that she was not going to be a party to this. She would not be his for the taking, regardless of what she'd let happen just moments ago.

But as Logan drove away, she knew her silent protests had a hollow ring to them. Time was running out—a fool could have sensed that much—and she was no closer to leaving Rachel than before.

It didn't take Logan's conscience long to become his worst enemy. By the time he arrived at his office, it was eating Swiss-cheese-size holes in his stomach.

Sure, he reasoned, technically he hadn't done anything wrong; he was a free man, Meredith was an unattached woman. But if he looked at the matter from an ethical and moral standpoint—and he always did—he had to admit he'd bulldozed over so many fine lines of judgment that he'd effectively turned that lily-white reputation he was known for in Rachel to a decidedly tainted gray.

Disgusted with himself, and more than a little afraid, he threw himself into his work with the energy and focus of a fanatic. Since there was no hope of avoiding Meredith, he decided his only solution was to preoccupy himself as much as possible, so that when he dropped into bed at night he'd pass out until his alarm sounded the next morning.

For the next week, he worked longer hours, took over responsibilities he would normally have delegated to employees, and generally succeeded in achieving his goal. By the end of every day, he was physically exhausted.

But as July eased into August, and the new school year fast approached, his contracts slowed down somewhat. So as not to feel undermined, he redirected his attention to the farm, noting that it was almost time for Sherman to harvest his next cutting of the alfalfa he raised for a few local dairy farmers. But when he offered his services, he discovered that, with Dan to help him out, Sherman didn't need him.

His nephew was also keeping the lawn mowed, he'd painted the picket fence out front, and he'd helped his grandmother clean out the attic, as she'd been wanting to do for months.

"Want to work out and practice some moves?" he asked his nephew upon arriving home early one Wednesday evening and following the boy to the barn as Danny put away some gardening tools for his grandmother.

"Gee, sorry, Uncle Logan, but I can't. I told Larry Brendan that I'd come over after dinner. His dad put up a hoop for him, and we're gonna shoot some baskets."

"Brendan...that's the family at the farm down the road?"

"Yes, sir."

"So you've finally made a friend at school?"

The boy broke into a shy smile. "I guess. It feels pretty good."

"Then I'm happy for you. Have a good time. Just don't come home too late, and be careful on the road."

Danny groaned. "Now you sound as bad as Gran and Mom. I haven't had dinner yet, and already you're giving me instructions."

"Nothing like staying consistent. Come on, let's go eat." But as they walked back to the house, he found himself mocking his intentions. *So much for your career as an uncle.*

Later, knowing he couldn't stay in the house with the sound of Meredith's voice reverberating through his head as she and his mother looked through old photo albums, he climbed into his truck and went for a drive. He double-checked his houses, although he already knew the crews had locked up as they should. He stopped to have a drink at the tavern at the motel on the highway. But when the bartender reminded him that he hadn't been there in a couple of months—not since he'd broken things off with Vanessa Calloway—that brought the painful realization of how long he'd endured his self-imposed celibacy.

But he did make it through the night, and the next and the next. By mid-August, however, a heat wave arrived unlike any they'd experienced in the past decade. Air conditioners worked overtime, and people tried to do as little as possible. Tempers exploded like pressure valves, and kids protested the wisdom of starting school if cooling systems weren't functioning. Most of all, *everyone* wanted someone else to cook dinner, and somehow Logan knew it was just a matter of time before his traditionalist mother, who'd failed to be pried away from her stove by a hurricane or tornado siren, surrendered, too.

"Let's barbecue," Faith said, upon his arrival home the second Tuesday of the heat wave.

At first Logan was game. He'd shut down the crews early and sent his office staff home, as so many businesses had to conserve energy. He didn't mind the prospect of being out in the heat because he figured Meredith would stay inside in the air-conditioning—a good thing, too, because she was wearing the cutoffs that sent his hormones into overdrive.

But then he realized his mother didn't mean for him to simply cook their meal outside.

"I've invited a few people over."

His goodwill melted faster than an ice cube in the sun. More people to witness his pretense that everything was all right and that he wasn't going systematically and completely out of his mind.

"Why?" he asked, as politely as he could.

"Because we haven't done anything like that in ages."

He couldn't argue with that. "Who's coming?"

"Sherman."

Sherman he could live with. They'd had him over to dinner many times. Holidays. The old guy's birthday...

"You'd better tell him the rest," Meredith added quietly, as she breezed by, carrying a large bowl of garden salad to the refrigerator for cooling.

Logan shifted his hands to his hips, increasingly unhappy. "Who else?"

"Stan Shirley."

He watched his mother empty a tray of ice cubes into the ice bucket. It wasn't a task that required such devoted concentration, but she was giving it the attention a safecracker would give Fort Knox. "Is this a belated April Fool's joke, or are you seriously conspiring to drive me nuts?" he asked, including Meredith in his glare. It wouldn't surprise him at all if she'd helped plan this to get back at him. He suspected his mother had told her of Stan's relationship to his ex-wife, and that Stan hadn't had much to say to him since Jane moved out.

"The heat's getting to your disposition, Logan," his mother said with an arched eyebrow. "Contrary to what you think, not everything that goes on in this house has to meet with your approval. Stan and I have been friends for a long time, and I don't see why I can't have him over to my home if I want to."

"There's no reason at all, except that you've never been inclined to do it until now."

"That's precisely the reason. It's ridiculous for a single man to have to cook for himself, especially in this weather. Besides, we'll all be working for the environment this way."

"You're reaching, Mother."

"I know it, but I thought I'd get your mind off the fact that Stan and Jane are related so I could also tell you that we ran into Mike LeBlanc at the grocery store. He spotted Merri, and one thing led to another...."

"Jane's *cousin?* Why didn't you invite her parents, too?"

"Don't be silly. Besides, they're in Georgia, helping Jane and her husband clean up after those terrible storms." After a dismissive wave, she carried the emptied ice trays to the sink for refilling. "Anyway, since Mike's an old classmate of Merri's, and a widower, I thought they might be good company for each other."

Logan stood scowling even after his mother picked up a tray of paper plates, the ice bucket and the silverware and carried it outside. Meredith ignored him and continued working, now stripping corn husks to be buttered and wrapped in foil for the grill. But after another moment or two, having his full attention finally won a reaction.

"It wasn't my idea," she told him, "so stop drilling holes into me."

"You didn't give LeBlanc the time of day in school." It made him sound like a jealous jerk, but Logan couldn't help it.

"Actually, if you care to think back correctly, it was the other way around. I was too weird for someone as strait-laced and conservative as him."

"What's the appeal now, the fact that he's a deputy sheriff? Since when did a uniform turn you on? It certainly didn't when I wore one."

"I shouldn't dignify that with any comment, but for your information, Buster, your mother felt sorry for him when she saw him reaching for TV dinners at the supermarket. That's the only reason he's coming.'' She ground the words out, shaking a wrapped ear of corn at him.

But Logan held on to his theory that a good meal wasn't the reason LeBlanc was joining them for dinner. He decided he was right only minutes after the cop arrived.

Mike's gaze followed every move Meredith made—not that Logan could blame him, since she was also wearing a peasant blouse that was about as substantial as a spider's web and exposed her creamy, fine-boned shoulders to the point of distraction. But it infuriated him that the guy barely tried to hide his interest.

By the time they sat down at the picnic table to eat—at which point Logan wanted to knock the supposedly shy law officer on his butt for claiming the spot beside Meredith— he couldn't have swallowed a bite of food if his life depended on it. First he'd had to deal with Stan's cool greeting, and now this.

And as if that weren't bad enough, his mother looked positively radiant sitting next to Stan. *Friend, my foot.* How long had they been making calf eyes at each other? he wondered sourly. How serious had it gotten? He frowned down at his food, which he'd turned into something a blender couldn't have pureed better.

"Isn't that right, Uncle Logan?"

Hearing his nephew say his name, he glanced over at Danny. "Sorry, what did you say?"

"My goodness, dear," his mother said, eyeing him with no small amount of concern. "You're certainly preoccupied tonight."

"Thinking about something at one of my projects, that's all." He forced a smile for his nephew. "Is what right?"

"What you said about me being a quick study? I was telling Deputy LeBlanc about the cool self-defense moves you taught me. Did you know my uncle got a Purple Heart and a Silver Star in Vietnam, sir? He's one tough dude.''

Son of a gun, Logan thought. Normally he liked to forget about those days, but he could have hugged the kid for mentioning it now. Apparently Dan had noticed LeBlanc's reaction to his mother, and didn't like it any better than *he* did.

''The whole town knows about Logan,'' LeBlanc assured Dan with a quiet smile. ''He's quite the hero around Rachel, but he's modest, too. He's never let the town honor him at any of its veterans' ceremonies. I'll bet he never told you that.''

How could he cut the guy down to size if he was going to be so damned polite? Annoyed, Logan spent the rest of the evening wondering what LeBlanc was up to. He knew the guy didn't like him; if they passed each other around town, they simply pretended the other one didn't exist. Maybe the cop had fooled Meredith, but not him.

What didn't slip past Meredith, however, was what he'd wanted to do to her guest. At the first opportunity, she sent Logan a look that promised retribution.

Anytime, anywhere, he thought, holding her gaze. In the end, she was the one to surrender and look away. But it left Logan feeling surprisingly more cheerful, and he turned to Sherman and began discussing the pending new farm legislation.

Meredith had conceded defeat to Logan during dinner, but the subject was by no means closed. She'd simply accepted that it would be wiser to wait to speak her piece. If the truth be known, however, she would have loved to throttle Logan the moment she witnessed his foolish display of male muscle-flexing at dinner.

Thank goodness for maturity and patience, she thought hours later, as she hovered by her bedroom door and listened to Faith closing the door to her own bedroom. In the old days, she would never have managed to restrain herself so successfully.

Logan had gone to bed several minutes ago, and Danny had turned in only moments before Faith. Merri waited another minute, then opened her door and stepped into the hall, dark now except for the night-light in the main bathroom. About to step across to Logan's room, she heard another door open.

"Mom?"

"Yes? What's wrong?" she whispered.

"I need to ask you something."

"*Now?*"

"Well, I wanted to earlier, because if you were gonna say no, I didn't want to be embarrassed in front of everyone. Larry's asked me to spend the weekend with him and his family. His folks are taking him to New Orleans as an early birthday present, and said he could take a friend if he wanted. He asked *me,* Mom. Can I go? He said we'd see the aquarium and take a riverboat ride, and best of all, his folks are paying for everything!"

She'd never seen Danny happier or more hopeful. It seemed he had made a good friend at last. How wonderful it would be to know she could stop worrying about his lack of rapport with people his own age.

"This weekend?" she whispered back. "Well . . . I know your grandmother respects and likes the Brendans. Are you sure you won't have any homework, or some report to do?"

"*Mom,* it's the first week of school. Even if a teacher assigns us something, I'll have time."

"Uh-huh." Did he realize she wouldn't sleep until he was home again? Except for the hours he spent in school, they'd never been apart before. But what an opportunity this was for him. "You really like Larry, don't you?"

"Yeah, he's pretty cool. Please, Mom. Can I?"

Wanting to hug him tight, Merri settled for touching his shoulder. "All right. You can tell him it's a go."

Barely stifling a whoop of delight, he hugged her. "Thanks, Mom, you're the best! I'm going to go downstairs and call him."

"At this hour?"

"It's only ten o'clock. He has a phone in his room, and he messes with his computer until eleven. G'night!"

"'Night."

Merri watched him race down the stairs. Belatedly she realized she'd missed the opportunity to talk to him about his part in trying to scare off Mike LeBlanc. Something needed to be said about jumping to conclusions, despite her understanding of the concern, even fear, that had led him to act possessive and protective of her. Under the circumstances, however, that could wait for tomorrow.

She stood there until she saw the glow from the kitchen light add to the illumination in the hallway. Then she turned toward Logan's room—and found him standing there watching her. Goodness, she thought, touching a hand to her throat. She hadn't heard a thing.

He joined her in the hallway. "Nice kid," he mouthed softly.

"I think so." As she gazed up at him, she became aware of his size, the fact that he'd removed his shirt, and that he had the well-developed body of a man decades younger. "We need to get a few things straight," she whispered back at him.

"Do we?"

"Don't use my son to play games with me."

"I'm not playing a game with you. Just stay away from LeBlanc."

The audacity of the man! She thought about telling him that he had no right to tell her who she could or could not see, but decided that was irrelevant. "I'm not interested in him. I'm not interested in anyone. Including you."

"Liar. Want me to prove it again?"

If he touched her, especially now, when he stood half-naked like that, she didn't know how well she could pretend he didn't affect her—or for how long. "No."

But as if he hadn't heard the strangled word, Logan reached out and took hold of the braided string weaving the neckline of her blouse together. Slowly he tugged the bow knot loose. The silky threading became a lover's caress as it brushed against her sensitive skin...until the last frayed ends fell free to her waist.

Her shirt slipped farther off her shoulders, and she felt cool air brush over the swell of her exposed, feverish skin. Surely this was a bluff, she told herself as she pressed a hand to her heart to keep her blouse up. He wouldn't do anything more. Not mere yards away from where his mother slept...

No sooner had she reassured herself, however, than he reached out and brushed his thumb across her lower lip. She took a cautious step back.

"Chicken."

"Sane. Let's stop this, Logan. I promise I'll try not to annoy you again."

"Too late. You're twenty-five years too late...and I'm not going to stand by while you make another mistake."

He'd taken another step toward her, and to offset it, she took another back. When she came flush against the doorjamb, she reached behind her to steady herself. "Another mistake?"

"Choosing the wrong man."

She opened her mouth to tell him he was mad. But she didn't get one consonant out before he swooped down and covered her mouth with his.

She was lost. Merri knew it the instant she felt herself sway on her feet, and she could no more have resisted kissing Logan back than she could have kept from taking her next breath.

Their lips fused, and their bodies—hardly compatible in size or build—locked together like two magnets. Within seconds she knew nothing but the power of him, his power over her, and her craving for more.

"Let's go into your room...or mine. I don't care which," he muttered against the side of her neck.

She didn't care either and, thankfully, that brought a surge of fear. What kind of woman was she, that she could become this wanton, this quickly? A muffled sound from downstairs also reminded her that her son would be coming up shortly, and that brought a greater clarity to her emotion-driven mind.

"Logan...Danny."

Exhaling shakily, he lifted his head. Merri used the opportunity to shove him with all her might and rush into her room, then shut the door and lock it. She almost failed. For a big man, he was fast on his feet, reminding her of his football days. He tried to stop her. But—apparently sane enough to be unwilling to make a great deal of noise—he didn't use all his strength.

She heard his sigh through the hardwood as he remained there for several more seconds. Pressing her cheek against the door, she felt a vibrant tingling as he slid his palm to the exact spot on the opposite side. Then he retreated to his room, and she finally heard the soft click of his door closing.

Exhaling, she slumped against the cool wood. She shook inside and out from the close call. Not since she was a child had she felt vulnerable in her own bedroom. But for the first time she knew her enemy was herself, every bit as much as that man.

Merri backed to her bed and crawled upon it. Snatching up her pillow, she buried her face against it and moaned in shame and in anguish over a hunger that must never be satisfied.

Five

***

By Friday's lunch rush, Merri realized something fateful was working against her. She'd already sensed the difference when she said goodbye to Danny the night before, as he packed and left to sleep over at the Brendans in order for them to get a quick start out of town immediately after school let out. There was something in the air, like the hum a telephone makes when the receiver's left slightly off the hook and one walks around the house wondering, *What is that sound?*

Merri finally realized that it was a plot to test her sanity when, during the noon rush at the café, as she was delivering four club sandwiches to a table of seven elderly ladies who'd already strained her patience with complaints, Faith phoned. Only the thought that Faith would never call unless there was an emergency had Merri hurrying to the phone instead of the first aid box, where the aspirin were kept.

"What's wrong?" she gasped breathlessly into the receiver. She signaled to the bankers who motioned for a refill of their iced tea.

"I'm so sorry to call you at work, dear. But I've just had some bad news."

Oh, Lord. "It's not Danny, is it? Did something happen at school? He has my number here. Why didn't he—"

"No. It's Stan."

For a moment, Merri's mind remained a blank slate. "Who? Oh! Your Stan." But, although she'd noticed the real and deep affection between the two the other day, Merri couldn't begin to imagine why Faith would call her about him during the café's busiest time. "What's the matter with him?"

"He was in a car accident, and he's broken his leg. I'm going to go stay with him for a few days to help him adjust to things."

"You're kidding?"

"He didn't ask, but it's the least I can do, since the accident happened right in front of our place. He realized he'd forgotten to deliver something up the street and made a U-turn without looking. Well, who would have thought there would be traffic on our road? Of course, it didn't help that he'd been preoccupied with talking to me."

"Merri! Your double side orders of fries and onion rings!" Angel called from the kitchen. They were for the truckers at table six, but she barely heard him.

"That's terrible news, Faith, and I hope he's okay otherwise, but I still don't understand why you—"

"Well, Danny's gone, and you and Logan can survive without me for a weekend. Stan doesn't have anyone, dear. Most of his relatives live out of town, and Mike has to work. My being gone won't cause a problem, will it?"

Now there was an understatement. Of course it would. The mere notion of being alone at the house with Logan for one night, let alone an entire weekend, had Merri feeling the first waves of a panic attack.

"It's not as though I'm going far, dear. Stan lives only seven miles or so from the house."

Seven or seven hundred, what did it matter? The point was, Faith wouldn't be sleeping in her own bed, and by her presence keeping Logan in *his*. "Of course there's no problem," she forced herself to reply. "Ah…don't worry about us. But are you sure you won't need an extra hand? I'd be happy to help in any way I can."

Faith vetoed the offer outright. "Stan's efficiency apartment is tiny enough as it is. I just needed to hear that you were okay with my decision."

Mars would be colonized before that was possible, but Merri knew Faith didn't want to hear that. Nor did she want to listen to Merri worry that after an incredibly slow start, things were moving awfully fast between her mother-in-law and Stan. Who was she to verbalize such a thought?

Angel leaned out from the kitchen. "Hey, Short Stack! You go deaf on me or something?"

Merri groaned. "I have to get back to work, or Angel will throw me in the walk-in cooler. So tell me quick, when are you leaving? Do you want me to find another ride home?"

"No need. As soon as I hang up with you, I'll phone Logan. I'm going to arrange for him to pick you up."

"No!" Merri cried, not caring how anxious she sounded. "Really, Faith, don't put yourself out. Besides, he'll just be getting back from his own lunch. Let's not upset him."

"When do I ask him for a favor? Once I explain that having peace of mind over you will allow me to get over to Stan's that much sooner, he'll understand. At any rate, he can't possibly blame any of this on you. Don't worry."

Logan could justify anything. But, seeing her truckers getting restless, Merri knew she had to get off the phone. "All right, Faith. We'll adapt to whatever you feel you need to do." And she would get through it taking one challenge at a time.

The rest of her shift passed in a blur, and by the time she saw Logan's pickup out front, she'd worked herself into such a knot of nerves that her stomach ached. She would have given anything not to have to walk outside and get into his truck. But because she'd made a few mistakes after Faith's call, she knew Angel was more than ready for her to go home.

As she exited the building, she could feel Logan's tension as easily as she felt her own. He sat staring straight ahead, and yet she sensed a feeling of triumph in him, too.

He didn't say a word as she climbed into the vehicle, nor did they speak the entire trip to the house. Words seemed unimportant at this point. After all, what could be said, and what difference would that make to the outcome? She knew what was happening as clearly as if he'd just spelled it out to her.

Only when they arrived at the house and Logan shut off the engine did Merri realize she had to have one question answered to be certain. "Are you going back to work?"

"No."

In the distance, she saw Sherman on his tractor, towing away a fallen tree from the edge of a field. Even if he finished his daily chores before evening, he wouldn't intrude. He lived his own life, kept his own schedule, and enjoyed his freedom. As for Danny, he was already on his way to New Orleans with the Brendans. No one, absolutely no one, would disturb them once they were inside. No one would stop them, which was exactly what she knew Logan wanted.

Merri felt more than heard him follow her into the house. The sound of him setting the lock had her straining for breath as if she'd sprinted home. Faced with an unexpected surge of cowardice, she made a beeline for the stairs.

The moment she put her hand on the banister, he was behind her, and laid his over it. Merri froze, stared. He was so big, so much darker, so much more powerful. What chance did she have if she tried to resist him?

He slid his other hand around her waist and drew her back against his hard body. She could feel his heartbeat, as well as his arousal, but it was when he shifted his right hand upward to cover her left breast that she knew her resistance was truly deserting her.

Weak-kneed, she let her shoulder bag drop to the floor, and as Logan stroked his thumb again and again over her pebbling nipple, she had to grip his forearm to remain standing. Somehow, the caresses through her clothes seemed more personal and erotic than if she'd been nude, so when he restlessly slid his hand downward to the juncture of her thighs, she dropped her head back against his shoulder and whimpered.

"I want your mouth," he murmured gruffly, his hot breath scorching her cheek. When she didn't comply, his touch grew more intimate. "Kiss me."

At the double assault on her senses, she lifted her chin and met his heavy-lidded gaze. "Logan . . . we can't do this."

"We already are. Turn around," he added, coaxing her. "Put your arms around me. Kiss me."

Mesmerized by the rough velvet of his voice, as much as by his touch, Merri obeyed as if in a trance. Nevertheless, she couldn't help adding, "There'll be no going back."

"I've lived in the past too long. I'm tired of the view."

"But tomorrow . . ."

"Doesn't exist. There's only now. This." They were thigh to thigh, mouth to mouth, and his arms had become steel bands drawing her closer. "Kiss me."

There was something exciting about being in Logan's control, a darker romance because he made choice and logic vanish. She knew she would be a full partner in what was about to happen; but it would be a Meredith Brown Powers who had never existed before. Logan would create her, and she accepted that reality even as she rose on tiptoe and gave him what he wanted.

This was their first kiss. The others had been duels, challenges . . . half-realized dreams. Punishments, too. This one was the acceptance of the energy that flowed unharnessed between them. Gone was the anger, the resentment, the doubts, the frustrations. As if they were longtime lovers, she parted her lips for the deeper joining that she sensed he didn't want to delay, and then there was only the familiarity, the pleasurable confidence, of sharing something wildly lush and uniquely their own.

Their tongues tangled in a pagan dance that went on and on, turning them into liquid beings, and it wasn't enough. Logan drank from her as if he were dying of dehydration, and that only created a demand for more. Groaning, he molded her closer, closer, from shoulder to thigh, as if he wanted to weld her body permanently to his, only to realize that wasn't enough, either.

With one arm around her shoulders and another beneath her hips, he lifted her against him. It seemed the most natural thing in the world to kick off her tennis shoes and wrap her legs around his waist. The movement had her skirt riding higher, which soon had Logan shifting again to caress her bottom with his big, demanding hands.

Muttering something unintelligible, he climbed up one step. By the second, she began to tug at his shirt. On the third, she had him out of it. They never broke their kiss, not even when he sank to his knees and set her on the step above him.

Then she felt his fingers on the buttons of her uniform. They moved rapidly—and not with excessive patience—until she could shrug out of the dress while he attended to the front closure of her bra. Cool air swept over her, countered by Logan's hot gaze. Eager for this next exploration by his hands and his mouth, Merri sank back against the stairs above them, only to arch toward him at the first touch of his steamy breath on her.

Frissons of exquisite pleasure shot through her as Logan worshiped, wet her and then provoked her until she buried her hands in his hair and writhed restlessly beneath him. She wanted to feel him like this with all her body, and he not only understood, he clearly wanted it, too.

He resumed stripping her, leaving her to work on his belt and jeans. Occasionally their fingers tangled and their eyes met; for a moment there would be the tiny shock of realization, recognition, and wonder. *Who are you? How can this be?* Then, either afraid to learn the answers or too addicted to what they'd created to stop, they began again the possessive, inciting caresses.

Somehow, their maneuvering carried them up two more steps and left them completely naked. As Logan splayed one hand low across Merri's midriff, and used his other to part her thighs, her heart leapt to her throat, and she flung out her arms and reached for a handhold on the banister, a brace on the wall. She'd never felt more wanton or more alive. The instant she felt his touch at her core, she cried out in a helpless spasm of sweet torment. When he followed that with a more intimate caress, the world spun away in a kaleidoscope of color and sensation.

She soared, she wept, she pleaded for a release from the explosion building within her. It had been so long, too long, and as if to tell her the same thing, Logan directed her hand to him. She needed only to feel the size and power of him to be grateful for his thoroughness in readying her.

"Oh, please... I'm not sure—" she gasped, struggling to get enough air into her lungs.

"Easy," Logan said gruffly, and lifted her in his arms, as if she weighed nothing. Shifting slightly, he then brought her flush against the wall and pressed himself between her thighs. "Yes," he hissed as Merri held his shoulders more tightly and subtly shifted for their joining. "Take me. Do it. Now."

He helped her, but she felt his hands shake as he held her hips and eased her over him, heard his voice crack when he whispered raw encouragements and curses between kisses that were a sensual claiming of another kind. "Merri...Merri...that's it. Deeper."

"No more. I can't."

"Please. All of me."

If he hadn't made that slip with her name again, said it in that aching, desperate way, she might have insisted he'd asked for too much. But this touching exposure of his vulnerability made the fact that it had been a long time for her bearable. As suddenly as the discomfort began, it eased, thanks to a constrained but steady rocking of his hips that spawned a blossoming pleasure.

Increasingly desperate for more contact, Merri sought another kiss. Logan gave it to her, his aim as accurate and devastating as the sensations he was spawning inside her. Within moments, the seductive rocking evolved into slow, rhythmic thrusts that soon covered their bodies with a fever's slick sheen.

Certain that this time she would melt into nothing, Merri was slow to realize he was lowering her with incredible care to the landing at the top of the stairs. As she grew aware of the soft pile under her back, she reached for him, not wanting to lose their closeness for a moment.

"I'll be too heavy," he warned.

"I don't care. Hold me."

Drenched, and as tangled together as two people could possibly get, they clung tight to ride the fierce wave of passion that carried them into breathless territory. When Merri's moment came, Logan swallowed her cry with the same greed with which he'd claimed all her sounds. When he reached his climax, however, he remained silent. Yet Merri didn't feel cheated. How could she, when he buried his face in the curve of her shoulder and shook from the release as if he were coming apart at every pore?

It was enough, because it was more than she'd ever imagined possible between two people.

Hell, damn, and— Logan bit off the rest of his curse, just as he gave up wishing he could be one of those lucky souls who died during lovemaking. Anything would be easier than dealing with the ebbing rush of what he was feeling, while knowing he might never experience it again. But, most important, he didn't want to have to look into Meredith's eyes for fear of what he would see in their depths once she realized what she'd done.

Sweet heaven, if she told him that she hated his guts, he would go downstairs and slit his throat with the dullest knife he could find. Heck, yes, he'd meant to jump her bones the instant they got inside; but from there on out, it had been sheer fantasy come true. He'd wanted this so badly for so long. When his mother told him of her plans for the weekend, he'd known he would have to be a saint to keep his hands off Meredith. He was definitely not saint material.

Jeez...on the stairs, no less. It was a miracle he hadn't killed them both in a fall. God, she was small. He'd never admitted that he liked that about her, didn't know if he could do it now. If she were any less independent, any less a firebrand, he would be afraid to touch her. Men his size were a bit much for petite women. He imagined they would look ridiculous on a dance floor; probably put out his back for weeks, he thought, reluctantly shifting his weight to his forearms. But as he gazed down at her flushed, glowing face, his heart wrenched with unfamiliar emotions, and cravings reignited in the lower part of his anatomy.

Merri lifted her spiky, charcoal dark lashes. He watched her midnight blue eyes lose their dazed, dreamy glaze and focus on him.

"Now what?" she asked him, a little tentative.

"The truth?"

"I'm old enough to handle it."

He shifted his gaze downward, over the pert breasts bearing the marks of his five-o'clock shadow and suckling kisses. "We start all over again."

"You want a weekend affair?"

"I want you. Having you once doesn't begin to satisfy my appetite." He fingered her sweat-damp hair, realizing he no longer resented its short length. The style suited her, as it would few women. He liked the way it curled around her face when it was wet. "What do you want?"

"The truth?"

Amused that she'd managed that with a straight face, he almost smiled. "I'm old enough to handle it."

"To understand you."

An ambitious request...and an enchanting one. But sometimes he didn't understand himself; how could he begin to explain who he was or what drove him to her? Granted, she wasn't the enemy he'd once believed, but could they ever be friends?

"You understand me, sexually," he murmured, brushing her damp hair from her forehead. "That's more than any woman's managed. Can't that be enough?"

"And come Monday?"

In Vietnam, a weekend had been a lifetime. It would probably have to be this time. As for what was going on in that sexy mind of hers, her expression didn't expose much, but he sensed her doubt. "Go on, get it out of your system."

"You're flirting with danger, Logan. People who play games often have them backfire on them."

He shook his head. "I'm not playing games. And I'm sure as hell not flirting. Call this...old business, if you like."

"I see. Hoping to cure what ails you, is that it?"

Hearing it put that way, he felt a moment's spasm of shame. He had to remind himself that Meredith had never been anyone's doormat. "Maybe we'll be doing both of us a favor," he said, knowing only that they had to come to some decision. He wanted her again, and if she waited much longer to tell him to go to hell, he was going to embarrass himself.

"I have one request," she replied, combing her fingertips through the mat of hair covering his chest.

Though he loved the feel of her hands on him, he remained wary as he nodded. "I'm listening."

"No more carpets. At least not today. As it is, I'll be lucky not to have a burn running the length of my back."

Her cheeky wit always used to incite him to fury. Now his chest shook momentarily with silent laughter.

Careful not to crush her, he rose, sweeping her into his arms in the process. "How do you feel about shower stalls?"

Instead of telling him, she showed him.

After the shower, Logan carried her to his bed, because it was the largest, and because he wanted nothing to do with any room that bore the barest trace of his brother, or Meredith's life with him. There they made love a third time before sleep finally claimed them.

It was dark when Logan awoke. For a moment it didn't faze him that he was alone. Only when his mind registered his body's pleasant fatigue and his senses picked up Meredith's clean, womanly scent on the pillow next to him did he remember.

His heart began to pound, as much at the memory of what they'd shared as in concern for where she might have gone. Could she have decided she'd made a mistake, and left?

Without Dan? Don't be an ass.

He pushed himself off the bed and took a clean pair of jeans from his closet. Barely taking time to slip them on, he headed into the hall without bothering to do more than zip them up halfway.

Her room was dark, but empty. So was the bathroom. But by then he saw the light coming from below. On his way down the stairs, he realized two things—she'd been busy picking up their clothes, and a delicious aroma was rising from the kitchen. A quick glance at his watch told him what his stomach already had; it was well past dinnertime, and he was starved. But the minute he stepped into the kitchen, his thoughts of food became secondary.

Meredith had dressed haphazardly herself. She wore the shirt he'd abandoned on the stairs, and, judging from the way she stood silhouetted against the stove light, not much else.

"Couldn't sleep?"

Gasping, she spun around. "How long have you been standing there?"

"Long enough to appreciate the view." He liked it from the front, too. She'd left her top three buttons open, which gave him a welcome reminder of skin that tasted smoother than cream, and sweet curves that made his fingertips itch. "You could have helped yourself to a clean shirt."

"Why waste Faith's ironing? Besides . . ."

She paused, and he wondered what she was suddenly hesitant to say. "Go ahead. Out with it."

"This one smelled like you."

She definitely knew how to keep him focused. He drew in a slow, deep breath. "Come here."

"I didn't mean to make that sound provocative."

"I forgive you, but come here anyway."

Her lips twitched as she crossed the room. The self-consciousness he'd sensed before was gone. Now her gem-bright eyes glowed with curiosity and remembered passion. Those eyes reminded him of the earrings she'd been wearing the last time he saw her, and he wondered what had happened to them. There'd been no sign of them since she arrived. But as soon as the thought came, he pushed it away. This was their weekend, he reminded himself, snaking an arm around her waist. There was no room for ghosts.

He lifted her until they were nose to nose. "Kiss me."

"Making love certainly didn't smooth out any of your rough edges."

"For a good reason. I want to make sure you can still recognize me in the dark," he drawled, an instant before capturing her mouth.

The kiss flared quickly to eager rediscovery. This was the pleasure that came with familiarity, Logan thought, wondering how many times he would have to draw her lower lip lightly between his teeth before he stopped enjoying the shivery response it elicited from her. He also wondered, if he swept away the paper plates and silverware from the table and replaced them with her trim tush, would he ever be able to enter this room again without getting hard?

"Logan. The food's going to burn."

He allowed himself one more sensual stroke of his tongue against hers before ending the kiss. But he consoled himself with letting her slide down his body as he set her on her feet. "Lucky for you I'm famished."

"Lucky for you there was leftover brisket in the refrigerator," she replied, her voice not much steadier than her body. "I'm not a creative cook after nine o'clock at night. I hope you don't mind chopped-beef sandwiches?"

He relished his effect on her. "It's better than the chunk of cheese and a rolled-up slice of bologna that I'd be getting for myself. If you add a beer to the menu, I promise to do the dishes."

A wicked light began dancing in her eyes. "You'll do them anyway. These are the nineties, mister... and I'm not your mama."

Laughing, Logan pulled out a chair and straddled it to watch her. When she handed him one of the two cans of beer, he popped the tab and took a long, necessary drink. After Meredith set her can by her place, she returned to the stove for the bag of hamburger buns, then the skillet of steaming beef.

"Chips? Pickles?"

He shook his head. She'd prepared enough brisket to feed three people.

"Onions?"

"Not unless you like the flavor." Again enjoying the aware look that returned to her eyes, he nudged out her chair with his bare foot. "Sit."

She sat. "There's no neat, let alone polite, way to eat these," she said, filling a bun until it was oozing. Adding the top half of the bread, she glanced up at him. "I thought you were hungry."

"I am."

"That was a hint. You're supposed to eat now. If you watch me as if I'm a specimen under a microscope, it'll make me end up with even more sauce on my chin."

"Don't worry. I'll lick it off."

She closed her eyes briefly. "I walked straight into that one. All right, let me ask you this—are we going to talk, eat and sleep around the subject of sex all weekend?"

"It's a strong probability."

"How long *has* it been for you?"

"How long has it been for *you?*"

She didn't respond right away. Logan realized too late that the subject hurt deeply, but despite the playful tone that had precipitated the subject, he was dead serious.

"Brett lost interest in sex some time before he was diagnosed. It might have been a symptom, or it just might have been me."

"Bull."

She shrugged. "He wouldn't have been the first creative person to burn up his passion in his work. He was an affectionate man otherwise. What else can I think?"

"That he was a double fool."

"You're very kind to my ego," she murmured, picking up her sandwich again. "That's difficult to get used to. You being kind to me."

"If you'll look at it as honesty, it'll be easier to swallow. And while we're on the subject of our response to each other, we'd better discuss birth control, don't you think?"

Meredith lifted a dark, finely arched eyebrow. "A belated concern, don't you think?"

Logan narrowed his eyes as she licked sauce off each finger of her right hand. She managed to make the smallest things provocative. "It goes to show you what hell you are on my common sense."

"Well, if it's any consolation, I doubt we have a problem. It was difficult enough to conceive Danny. My doctor told me it would be nothing short of a miracle if I managed to get pregnant again. He must have been right. We did try, and it never happened."

"Are you sorry?"

"I believe in the saying about things working out for the best. Sometimes it was damned hard to keep just the three of us warm and fed."

For years Logan had tried not to think about that. If Brett had been the way he was here, what had he been like out in the world? As a husband? As a father? The potential answers that came to mind weren't pretty.

Meredith shook her head, as if to cast off her own dark thoughts, and summoned a smile for him. "What about you and Jane? Did you two ever want children?"

"We never discussed it." Every year there was less and less to say about his marriage. "We never discussed much of anything."

Nodding, Meredith pursed her lips. "Did you make her salute you when you drove off to work in the morning?"

"Don't get cocky. I can admit my mistake in thinking a wife would fix everything for me. I guess I should have known I'm the type of guy who should stay away from marriage."

Meredith uttered a deep-throated sound of skepticism. "Most men try on that logic...until they meet the right woman."

"Were you the right woman for Brett?"

Once again she hesitated, fingered the letters on her beer can. "I believe so. For a while. I know you didn't agree."

"I still don't."

She searched his face, her expression as perplexed as it was sad. "How can you work at disliking me so much and yet make love to me the way you do?"

He set down his barely touched sandwich and ruthlessly wiped his mouth with his napkin. "One has nothing to do with the other. And at the risk of getting that pan turned over my head, maybe you should be careful in labeling what we've been doing."

Meredith almost succeeded with her mocking smile, but her eyes were overbright. "No one will ever mistake you for a romantic, will they, Logan? But it is interesting to note that if we sidestep discussing everything you're touchy about, we're going to have as little to say to each other as you and Jane did."

Two hits in a row. If he wasn't careful, her next shot might be fatal.

"Fine," he said, rising and sweeping her up from her chair before she could react. He kissed her soundly for good measure.

"What are you doing?" she gasped when he let her breathe again.

"Fogging up your cross hairs."

"In English, please."

"Talking will just waste the time we have left, so let me put it this way. I've wanted you for a long time. Now I have you." The devil with what she'd make of that, he thought, starting for the stairs.

"But—" As he took them two at a time, Meredith wrapped her arms around his neck. "Logan—the food!"

"Some things can wait. This can't."

wrapped her arms around His neck. "Merry—the baby! Where can it be?"

Six

"Are you sure you're all right?"

Merri cradled the telephone receiver between her shoulder and ear, and decided that for all her tender, loving ways, her mother-in-law had the shrewd and keen instincts of a hawk. "Of course, Faith. Why on earth do you ask?"

"You sound tired . . . and a little depressed."

Considering the fact that she'd just lived the fullest two days of her life, and that the fantasy was about to end in a few hours, she figured she had a reason to be exhausted. As for feeling depressed, well, she was that, too. Because as good as things had been between her and Logan on one level, she'd never felt more uncertain as to what the future held.

"I'm missing two of my favorite people in the world," she managed, trying to add some amusement to her voice. "That's all."

"You're sure you're not hiding something? Like maybe that Logan's been more difficult than I'd feared? If so, tell me the truth, dear. I warned him about being fair to you."

Fair. Oh, he'd been that, all right. He'd been as generous a lover as he'd been complete. Intense. She was the one with the problem.

"I guess you're hearing my worry about Danny," she said, since that at least was true. "He hasn't called since Saturday morning."

"Ah…I understand. He's having the time of his life, and has forgotten about everything else. A mother's nightmare," Faith intoned, a smile in her voice. "I remember the first time that happened with my boys. Do you know, I hid in my room and cried like a baby, then got so disgusted with myself, I went downstairs and baked six dozen chocolate chip cookies? An hour later, both boys were back and arguing across the kitchen table about whose cookie had more chips. Keep your chin up, dear. Everything will return to normal shortly."

Who wanted that? Of course, she didn't have a clue as to what she *did* want. Knowing she needed to get off that subject, she asked, "How's Stan coming along?"

"He's a nurse's dream," Faith gushed. "I'll never be able to deal with a cantankerous patient again."

This time Merri laughed easily. "Watch out, you sound smitten."

"That's not the half of it. We'll talk when I get back. Right now he's waiting for the beer I promised him. See you right after I make him dinner, dear."

Merri sighed as she hung up the receiver on the wall unit. A few more hours… She would be glad to have Faith home again, but there would be a high cost to her return.

The back door opened, and Logan entered. Merri quickly returned to the task of putting away the pail and mop she'd been using to clean up the bathroom and kitchen. She'd decided to do a bit of polishing right after Logan spotted Sherman having trouble with his old pickup and went out to help. At the least, she'd wanted to wash the bed sheets, not to mention the several towels they'd used. Naturally, though, the longer Logan had stayed with Sherman, the more things she'd seen that could be wiped down or spruced up.

"What's the verdict?" she called as he shut the door. "Will the truck last another year?"

"Not likely." Logan went to the sink and began washing his grit-covered hands. "But I already told him that whenever he's ready, I'll give him mine. It's taken me half my life, but I finally know better than to try and give him a completely new one. He's too proud for his own good. As it was, I had a hard time convincing him that despite its being only two years old, I'd already put forty thousand miles on mine, and that it wasn't too new to exchange for another one. He didn't completely buy that, but when I added that I relied on him to have an operational vehicle in case my mother had an emergency when I wasn't around, he finally relented."

This was a side of Logan that she'd never seen all those years ago. Oh, he'd been hardworking, and good to his mother; but his gestures had always come off more as bequeathals than as acts of kindness. Merri's heart filled with warm emotions at the compassion she was sensing for the first time. "That's so nice of you, Logan."

"Yeah, I'm a real sweetheart."

This sounded more like the old Logan, and Merri studied him, wondering if he had noticed the brief softening and was trying to hide it. Or had something else happened while he was outside? Oh, Lord…could Sherman have seen them together sometime over the weekend?

He didn't have to see anything, you ninny!

No, he didn't. She almost blushed when she realized they'd hardly stepped out of the house except to collect the mail and newspaper. That alone would have drawn suspicion. And what if he'd glanced in the kitchen or back door window when they were down here preparing a meal? Oh, dear. But surely Sherman wouldn't say anything to anyone. He respected the family's privacy too much, just as they respected his.

"I, um, just talked to your mother," she said, with determined brightness. "She sounds wonderfully upbeat for someone who's obviously been working all weekend."

"Good for her." Logan shut off the tap and wiped his hands. His back muscles flexed and stretched beneath his white T-shirt as he replaced the hand towel on its rack. "Did she say when she'd be coming home, or are we supposed to guess?"

What on earth—? She didn't get this mood at all. "Logan. I'm willing to get dinner, if that's what you're worried about. And it's not as if we can't reach her to find out—"

"Did I say I was worried?" Looking very much like a caged animal, he started out of the room, stopped, and then stood there as if he didn't know where he was, let alone what he was supposed to do. It was then that he sniffed, looked around the room, and noticed that she'd been busy, too. "Hell. You've done all the cleaning. I should have been in here helping you get things back into shape."

"You were busy yourself." She hadn't minded. What bothered her was seeing the tension and resentment building in him, and not understanding where it had come from or who it was directed at. "I thought I'd bake a cake to welcome home Danny and your mom. Can I get you a snack or something before I start?"

"No. Thanks, though."

"Sure? You haven't had anything since breakfast." Of course, they hadn't gotten out of bed until after *nine*, and she had the deliciously aching muscles to prove it. "Uh . . . why don't you get yourself a drink? You look—"

"Look, I don't need a nursemaid like Stan, all right? If I want something, I'll get it for myself!"

For endless seconds afterward, the room was so silent, Merri could hear the soft ticking from the round battery-operated clock above the refrigerator. If this was a taste of what she had to look forward to once the others returned, she wanted no part of it.

Turning on her heel, she headed upstairs, ignoring Logan's call. When he caught up with her at her bedroom doorway, she spun around to shake off his restraining hand.

"Let go! I don't know what's gotten into you, Logan, but I resent the artillery barrage being aimed at me."

"Merri . . ."

"And you can stop that, too. How dare you 'Merri' me every time you make a fool of yourself or decide you want me!"

"You're right. It's not only manipulative, it's shallow manipulation."

He said it so quietly, so earnestly, that at first she wondered if she'd heard him correctly. When convinced she had, she slumped back against the doorjamb in relief that he'd stopped. "Then why do it, Logan?"

"Because I'm fed up with myself. Disgusted with this situation. This isn't the way I planned the rest of our time together to be. I wanted—" He swore and raked a hand through his hair before giving her a resigned look. "I intended our last hours together to be different than this."

Their last hours . . . The words were incomprehensible. They left her feeling as if she were being sucked into some twilight zone from which she might never escape, destined to relive these same few days again and again. And what bizarre phrasing, when neither of them was going anywhere!

She'd thought—oh, not at first, but later—she'd *hoped* that what they'd shared would change things between them. Even yesterday, there'd been a glimmer of hope burning in her heart. Clearly she'd been wrong.

"The last few hours of what, Logan?" she asked, suddenly weary, and feeling more than a little like a fool. "The end of our romp, or fling, or . . . what *do* we call it? The end of the cease-fire? What happens tomorrow morning, when you drive me to work? Do we go back to being silent antagonists, as if this weekend never happened? When we sit across from each other at that table downstairs, are you going to pretend to forget how it was between us when we were the only ones in the house?"

"I don't know, all right? Damn it, I didn't plan this, and I don't have the answers any more than you do!"

What had they done? Merri stared at the man who was trapping her with his hands and glaring as if the whole thing were her fault. The stranger was returning, the Logan she'd never understood.

God . . . the recklessness of it, the insanity. Hadn't she learned her lesson from her mother years ago? She'd worked hard over the years to become the kind of person who always thought things through, to wipe out the recklessness and impulsiveness in herself. She'd succeeded, too . . . until this weekend. How ironic that Logan should be the one to help her create the granddaddy of messes.

She averted her head, unable to look at him a moment longer. When she felt his knuckles caress her cheek, she could hardly bear it.

"Don't," he entreated hoarsely. "I'm sorry for losing it. I don't want to fight."

"Me neither."

"It's just . . . I can't promise you anything."

She lifted her chin. "Did I ask you to?"

"No. But in a way I wish you would."

"Why? To ease your conscience? That's not necessary, Logan. We're both consenting adults. Not very bright ones, it seems, but we didn't do anything wrong."

"Except that in a few hours we have to forget what we shared, because it would devastate my mother if she found out."

"And Danny," Merri added, leaning her head back against the wood of the doorjamb and letting her eyes drift shut.

"But this has been the most incredible weekend of my life. I'd hoped there was some way to let you know," he said, his voice a caressing rumble.

"It hasn't crossed your mind to just tell me?"

"I've never been good at talking to you."

That was true enough. She'd tried to strike up conversations with him throughout the weekend, but without much success—unless it was about the chemistry, the passion, between them. Her body came instantly alive as she remembered how eloquent he'd been at verbalizing what he wanted from her as a lover, and what she made him feel.

"Even now," he continued, "I know we should talk, but other things get in the way." Logan shifted to frame her face with his hands. "Being aware of all the disruption we could cause should make it easy to keep my hands off you. So why is it damned near impossible?"

Helpless not to, Merri met his brooding gaze. This was her lover. He wasn't a pretty or funny man, and he had neither a poet's soul nor an artist's eye for the beauty of the world around him. He was a warrior, a survivor. Whatever gentleness and tenderness remained inside him after his expe-

riences in the war were hidden behind thick armor. Lo̶
in the darkness of his soul, it would slowly wither, if it
wasn't already at the brink of extinction.

He was troubled and troubling. If she had an ounce of
sense, she would mark him down to experience and run, not
just walk, away from him. They weren't good for each
other. Something in their psychological makeup triggered
the most negative things in each other.

But, as with so many shadows from the past, she couldn't
escape him. Fate had insisted on reuniting them. When he
opened up even briefly, when he was honest with her, this
stubborn, strong giant of a man could touch her heart as no
one ever had. When his big, callused hands reached for her,
he owned her soul.

Crazy, she thought, seeing the embers of passion flicker
to life in his eyes again. When he inched closer and bent to
kiss her, despite the fluttering of excitement she felt in her
stomach, she touched her fingertips to his mouth.

"No more, Logan."

"Once more."

"Right or wrong, we had our time. But it's over."

Taking hold of her wrist, he kissed the spot where her
pulse beat too fast, then planted another kiss in her palm
before placing her arm around his neck. "Not yet, it isn't.
You know that, too. You can't even look at me now, because you know it's the truth."

He was right, which made her all the more determined to
avoid his gaze. If she let those penetrating eyes seduce her
again, she knew, he could take her standing right there, and
she wouldn't try to stop him.

But Logan was far more clever, as well as determined. He
didn't want her to succumb, he wanted her as an active par-
ticipant, and he knew exactly how to turn her tethered desire into unbridled passion.

to force her to meet his gaze, he began with kisses. Fleeting but hungry kisses that along her hairline, across her cheekbone, below the tip of her nose... again and again, until she felt her world begin to spin into a dizzy blur and her insides heat and churn into a steamy craving. Kisses everywhere but where she hungered for them the most—on her lips.

"What is it?" he whispered, as if sensing her frustration. "Tell me what you want."

She couldn't let him reduce her to this. Telling herself that she had at least an ounce of survival instinct left inside her, she clenched her hands and pushed against his hard chest.

Logan reciprocated by shifting his focus to the sensitive parts of her neck and throat. He was reminding her of late yesterday, when she'd turned out the last light downstairs, thinking he'd already gone up to bed. Instead, he'd surprised her by coming up behind her. He'd covered her breasts with his hands and pressed his mouth to the side of her neck. The things he'd done after that... Remembering, she felt herself tremble as if her legs had turned into warm putty.

"Come to bed with me, Merri."

"Downstairs...the door's unlocked. Anyone could come in."

"No one's going to come in. We have time."

He couldn't know that, not for sure. But as he slowly, determinedly, *finally* covered her mouth with his, she opened her fists to grab at his shirt as she would have at sanity. Then she felt herself being drawn down, down, into the nerve-stunning sea of sensations he alone controlled.

The next thing she knew, Logan was laying her across his bed and quickly pinning her there with his body, as if afraid she might make a run for it. But she had only to feel his familiar weight again, the possessive way he all but surrounded her, to understand the inevitability of this.

Maybe he was right. Maybe they needed to let their passion soar, if only to burn it out, to finish with each other so that they could continue with their lives without destroying one another.

By mutual consent, some inexplicable signal of the kind only lovers know, their next kiss grew into a torrid ravishment; hands and mouths streaked everywhere to feel and taste everything and at once. It was as if this were their first reunion in a year, instead of mere hours. With a groan, Logan rolled onto his back and drew Merri over him to drag off her top. Then it was his turn, and she rid him of his T-shirt. The pleasure of being flesh to flesh again drew everything from whispers to erotic sighs, as well as an eager determination to remove the rest of their clothes.

"You," Logan rasped, streaking a hand down her bare body. "You don't look as if you've given birth, let alone have a teenage son."

And he looked like the combatant he'd been. A modern-day gladiator, who she'd discovered bore other scars than the one on his chin. When he had her straddle him, she leaned down to place kisses on that terrible injury, and then on the various smaller trophies from battles and skirmishes that had turned him into an even harder, unyielding man.

Her caress to the bullet graze low on his right hip had him sucking in his breath sharply. She knew that if it had been a few inches to the left, it could have crippled him for life. A few inches higher, and Faith would have lost him well before she lost Brett.

For years the thought of him suffering, dying so young and alone in some foreign place, had been a thing she had refused to let herself think about. Now it all came rushing at her like the deadly bullets he'd become too well acquainted with. Shivering, she alternately stroked her cheek over and kissed the flat, taut plane of his stomach.

"Merri . . . sweet hell, you're killing me."

She didn't trust herself to speak, to let him know what the marks on his body did to her. Instead, she came to his half-opened zipper and finished easing it the rest of the way down. His musky male scent had become as familiar to her as her own. So had touching him. She'd learned exactly what made him hot, and what made him crazy, and, releasing him to her questing touch, she showed him how well.

His breath caught on a ragged curse; the hands that cupped her head shook as he arched to get closer to her. It gave her a strange, exciting sense of power to feel this control she had over him. But no sooner had the heady thrill begun to build than he once again gripped her by her waist and dragged her upward.

"I want it to happen when I'm inside you," he rasped, his fingers testing her readiness. "I want to come watching you above me."

She wanted that, too. Anything. The pleasure of being with him, his hands on her, his eyes burning with unspoken thoughts as they memorized every inch of her.

She sank onto him carefully, tender from hours and hours of his insatiable hunger. The feeling of being possessed was beyond description. But she never said a word. She couldn't. It was too much to watch the passion and need in his face and know it was *her* he wanted. Besides, she was afraid of breaking the spell. If this was to be the last time, then she wanted him to carry the memory of it to his grave.

Combing her hands through her short hair, she closed her eyes as she began rocking against him. Slow, undulating movements, like those of an Eastern dancer. As she heard his breathing grow harsh and the pressure inside her build, she felt his almost painful grip on her hips, encouraging her to intensify the exotic dance.

There should have been wind, lightning and thunder. It was that stunning, that breathtaking. And when Merri felt Logan's shuddering release inside her, her body quaked with the spasms of her own ecstasy. Replete, she yielded eagerly as he crushed her against his heaving, damp chest.

A long, pulsating silence followed. Logan felt it stretch and build like an afternoon thunderhead as both of them resisted moving or speaking. It was inevitable, though; someone had to say what he knew was on both of their minds, and it wasn't going to go away.

"Heaven help us," he said, his throat as dry as it had been at any moment in those Southeast Asian jungles when death crept close. "We know we can't live *with* each other... but how the hell are we going to live *without* one another?"

He felt Meredith—Merri—take a deep breath, but she failed to make any comment. Well, he mused, why should she? It had been a rhetorical question; and if they hadn't been able to answer it up until now, what made him think anything had changed?

Worried, but strangely at peace, too, he stroked her hair. Maybe if he told her that he cared—? She had to know he did, but if he told her—

A noise from downstairs halted his thoughts. Merri stiffened.

"Mom? I'm home!"

A sound of absolute horror stayed strangled in Merri's throat, but her motor skills sprang to life. Wriggling out of Logan's arms, she sprang off the bed and onto her feet with the agility of a schoolgirl. Her expression horrified, she spun around, snatching clothes from every direction, and then bolted for the door.

"Get dressed, or lock this!" she whispered, closing the door behind her.

Logan raised himself up on one elbow. Beyond the door he heard the muffled sounds of Dan calling for his mother again, and from what he presumed was her room the sound of drawers opening and shutting hastily as she got dressed. Lucky for her she wore as little as she did, and dressed without any deference to haute couture. But his fleeting amusement quickly gave way to a pang in the vicinity of his heart.

Now their weekend had truly come to an end. Without any last words, or agreement—any attempt to reach beyond what they'd shared to find friendship.

Was fate working for or against them this time? He sure as hell wished it would make up its mind.

As he sat up and swung his legs to the carpet, he heard Merri race down the hall and call, "Danny? Is that you?"

Very realistic, he thought, not without a touch of bitterness. On the other hand, what did he want her to say? The truth? Then what?

"Your trouble is, you always think too much," he muttered, rubbing his face and reaching for his jeans. He needed to learn to simply go through the motions and get through the day.

But how are you going to get the scent of her, the taste of her, out of your system?

He was still trying to think of an answer as he descended the stairs. Excited chatter intervened.

"...and it was so cool. But most of all I liked the riverboat ride up the Mississippi. We saw everything! There were these old plantations, and then there were the eeriest cabins rising out of the water on telephone poles."

"Utility poles."

"Why don't they rot?"

"They're treated. When was the last time you saw a *telephone* pole rot? Right?"

"I guess."

"Usually when you do see them replaced, it's because the ground shifts, causing the pole to tilt badly. In some places they've been having problems with woodpeckers wearing them out, but short of a lightning strike or a tornado, that's all that's going to get them."

"Where did you learn all that?"

"I wasn't exactly hatched from an egg yesterday, my friend."

A muffled laugh followed. "You're making me forget my story. Anyway, along comes this humongous barge with stuff going who knows where. It was like watching a movie. So what did you do while I was gone?"

The muscles in Logan's abdomen clenched in anticipation.

"Oh, nothing as exciting as all that. Worked. Cleaned."

"Sorry I asked."

Sorry I listened. Logan knew she'd had to lie, but he couldn't help being annoyed that she'd done it so easily and so well.

"Hey, Uncle Logan! How're ya doing? I saw your truck outside, but I thought maybe you were out with Sherman."

The boy was a veritable bubble of adrenaline, and Logan found a real enough grin for the youngster. After all, he liked the kid, and it wasn't as if any of this mess were Dan's fault.

"No, I finished some paperwork a while ago, and it about wiped me out, so I took a nap," he said, feeling uneasy.

"Jeez, you're right, Mom. It was a real drag around here. I'm glad I got to escape."

Merri tugged the duffel bag from the teenager's grasp and carried it back to the washing machine. "That'll be all of that, Mr. Sophisticated World Traveler. I was about to start a cake, because your grandmother will be home soon herself, and I thought— Oh! You don't know, do you? Something did happen this weekend."

Logan began feeling like a square block trying to fit into a round hole. As Merri told him about Stan Shirley's accident, mother and son fell into animated chatter about the mail carrier, mostly at a speed Logan couldn't have kept up with even if a good chunk of his concentration weren't focused on and vulnerable to every movement Merri made. After almost a minute of finding no place to join in on the dialogue, he got himself a beer, intent on letting himself out the back door...if he could ease past Merri without making a fool of himself if their bodies touched. But when Merri did clear out of the utility nook, the door opened before he could get to it.

He stared at his mother's rosy, beaming face. "Aren't you early?" he asked, not caring how inane that sounded.

"Hello to you, too," Faith replied, handing him her overnight bag as she brushed past him. "Danny! You beat me. Hello, Merri, dear."

Logan watched his mother kiss Merri and hug her grandson. She hadn't done either to him, and it struck him that he couldn't remember the last time she had. He did recall that she always used to show affection to Brett. Of course, he would have been the first to insist he hadn't needed the coddling; he'd been the strong one in the family. So why did he feel surprise now? Why did it sting so much?

"After he listened to us talking, Merri, Stan got a guilty conscience and insisted on having take-out food for dinner so I could get back here and check on my family. A good thing, too. Meredith Powers, you look as if you haven't eaten a bite since I left. And you, my boy," she said, tousling Dan's hair, "I bet you've done nothing but eat junk food all weekend!"

"I had fried alligator for lunch yesterday."

As both women made the appropriate shocked responses, Logan absorbed the cozy scene and had no problem visualizing it five or even ten years from now. But, no matter how hard he tried, he couldn't see where he fit in the picture. It left him feeling emptier than ever.

No one noticed as he set his mother's bag on the floor and backed out of the room. He exited the house through the kitchen door and grimaced up at the hot afternoon sun.

All his life he'd felt like an outsider in his family, a third wheel. A part necessary to their survival, sure; but a part that had often been overlooked or taken for granted. When he was around the others, he'd been the straight man to Brett's charming scoundrel. In the end, when Brett ran from responsibility for the last time, he'd forced Logan into the role of the heavy.

Nothing had changed. What he'd shared with Merri had already been swept aside.

What was it about him that made people shut him out so easily? Why didn't anyone turn to him when it came time to laugh? Where were his hugs?

"Logan?"

Caught up in his thoughts, he didn't hear Merri come up behind him. Although his heart began pounding at the sound of her soft voice, he curled the hands in his pockets into fists to keep himself from being too pleased.

"Why'd you leave the happy reunion?"

"Your mother's gone upstairs to unpack. Danny's going to take a shower." She inched closer, her gaze concerned. "Are you all right?"

"Are you?"

"Not really. I feel as if I'm in a school play and I've forgotten my lines."

"Well, I'm no expert, but you seem a natural at winging it. You convinced me that you're glad to see them."

Her gaze held entreaty. "Come back inside. They'll miss you, and wonder."

"No, they won't. Besides, I don't have your ability to pretend."

She wrapped her hands around her waist. "Why are you being intentionally confrontational? I'm trying to—"

"Who asked you to?" Logan snapped, angry because he could still feel the sweet pressure of her body against his and wished he didn't. "Don't spread yourself too thin, honey. Go back inside and be the perfect mother and daughter-in-law. No one's asking you for anything more."

He'd never seen her turn so pale. Not even the amber sun could add color to her ashen skin. For an instant, he could have sworn a tear almost spilled over one of her dusky lashes. But when she stiffened, pivoted on her heel and went back inside without another word, he knew that if there had been a tear, it had merely been one of fury.

Now everything was *really* back to normal.

"Great," he muttered to himself. "That's just great."

Seven

"That's my tuna on rye, Toots," Maggie chided, snatching the green platter from Merri's hands.

"It is?" Merri glanced around in confusion until she intercepted Angel's pained look. "Well, I thought it was mine. Where's my order for tuna on rye?"

"Yours is tuna on a kaiser roll," the long-faced man replied. "And it's right here."

As he set the blue platter on the chest-level counter, Merri brushed her damp bangs from her brow with the back of her hand. Was she losing her mind? Of course she'd known table two had ordered the roll.

She offered Angel a weak smile. "Sorry."

"Don't be sorry, just get your act together. You've been walking around like a zombie for days. Beginning to look like one, too," Angel added, torpedo-shaped eyebrows threatening to collide over his thin nose. "You sure you're not coming down with something?"

"Nothing worse than sore feet." It wasn't exactly the truth, Merri admitted to herself as she delivered her order, but her life had enough tension at the moment; she didn't want to have to deal with questions and advice, too. Regardless of how good the intentions were. Her boss and co-workers, not to mention the rest of Rachel, Louisiana, didn't need to know that in the past several weeks she'd been living on an emotional fault line.

Logan had become withdrawn again, burying himself in work and using any and every excuse not to come home. When he did grace the house with his presence, he could barely bring himself to look at her—and forget about getting him to talk to her.

Once Faith noticed his increased reserve, she'd asked Merri if something had happened lately that she'd missed.

"Did you two have words on the way to work or something? He may be my son, but I'm not blind to his stubbornness and pride."

Merri had straddled the fine line between truth and deceit. "We don't talk in the morning, Faith."

At least they didn't usually have anything to say to each other. This morning he'd seemed to really look at her for the first time, and he'd all but snarled, "You look like hell."

She'd been equally sweet-tempered. "Well, I should! Listening to you trudge in at every hour of the night cuts into my sleep!"

Only Danny had any luck in getting him to unbend. When her son asked about the weights he'd discovered stored away in the barn, Logan had helped him to set them up, and had come home early several days in a row to show him and his friend Larry several routines to help them begin working out.

Merri had been touched and pleased. But having to listen to both boys gush about him soon became almost too much to bear. And her appreciation evaporated completely once she heard the boys talk of more self-defense lessons.

She knew, however, it wasn't just the violence and the male-bonding things. She was tired of pretending nothing had happened between her and Logan. She was slowly losing her mind from lying in bed at night remembering his kisses, the feel of his strong body possessing hers. But not all the things she missed about him were sexual.

She also missed the unfamiliar but welcome sense of well-being that came from being in his presence. Her—a woman who'd never let herself rely on another human being in her life, because none had ever been there for her. A woman who'd found it easy and acceptable to be married to whimsical, dreamy Brett, despite his unreliability as a breadwinner, because she knew she was the stronger one and that *he* needed *her.* Why had it all changed when she was with Logan that weekend?

Crazy, she thought for the dozenth time, that was what it was, and if she didn't get hold of herself soon, she was going to get seriously sick. She wasn't blind to the fact that she'd lost pounds she couldn't afford to lose because her appetite was gone and she wasn't getting enough sleep.

"Merri, girl...what on earth is your problem? If you give change for a twenty every time a customer gives you ten dollars, you're gonna bankrupt poor Angel before the month's out."

The usually patient Corinne's exasperated voice cut into Merri's brooding and had her staring at the money in her hand. "My God—I didn't realize."

What next? she wondered, as embarrassed as she was frustrated with herself.

By the end of the lunch rush, she'd decided she shouldn't have asked that question. With one waitress out for a family emergency and another sick, she and Corinne were splitting the two dozen tables between them. It meant nonstop running for nearly ninety minutes.

As the café began to empty, Corinne handed Merri a glass of iced tea and cornered her in the doorway of the supply room to make sure she took a sip. Merri did, because her throat was parched. She was grateful for the gesture—until she tasted the amount of sugar the brunette had heaped in the glass.

"Ugh! Corinne, what are you trying to do to me?"

"You need the energy. Drink."

"If I do, I *will* get sick."

"You'll get sick if you don't drink it." The tall woman dampened a paper napkin and dabbed at Merri's face. "Glory be, you're on fire, honey."

"We both should be. We just broke the four-minute mile about twenty times."

"Ain't that the truth! But seriously, you don't look good. I'd consider getting a checkup if I were you. Nowadays with all these weird diseases popping up in the news left and right, you can't be too careful."

But Danny needed to get to a dentist, he was beginning a welcome growing spurt, which would mean more clothes, and she was saving up for a car she'd seen at the used-car lot across the street. If she cut a few more corners, she might be able to afford it by Christmas. It wasn't much, as cars went, but it looked solid enough to get her to town and back until she could afford something better. At least she would be able to avoid Logan's cold shoulder. That change alone should begin easing some of the tension in her life.

"I'll make a point to get to bed early tonight," she told the other woman. "I promise." She brought the glass of tea to her lips to try and gain more approval, but her stomach revolted. Badly.

"What?"

Obviously her expression had given something away. "I'm just a little..."

Suddenly the room began to spin, the tea in her glass began to slosh over the rim from her violently shaking hand. Merri blinked and tried to make sense of it all, understood that she really needed to sit down.

"Merri?" she heard from a faraway place. *"Merri!"*

Logan broke every speed limit between the office and Rachel Municipal Hospital. The scary thing was, he barely saw any of the terrain he covered. He hadn't been aware of much of anything since getting the call from Angel's Café saying that Merri had fainted and an ambulance was coming to rush her to the hospital. He understood that the mind had a way of protecting itself; his rejected any emotion or reaction except what was necessary to get him where he needed to be.

God, what had happened? What was wrong? As he pulled into the emergency parking area, the questions hammered at him again and again, as violently as the blood pounding in his temples. If she was seriously ill— He couldn't bring himself to think about that.

Racing into the building, he was about to ask for information at the admissions desk when he spotted Angel. He muttered something incoherent to the nurse and made a beeline for Merri's employer.

Angel's curly, ear-length hair was in disarray, his black eyes were round with lingering shock, the skin across his heavily whiskered olive face was taut. Logan figured he looked at least that bad himself, but he didn't let that keep him from getting straight into the older man's face and to the point.

"What the hell is going on?"

"She fainted."

"Why?"

"Please. I'm no doctor, how should I know?"

"She works for you. You're around her all the time. you don't know, who should?"

A security guard came around the corner and scowled them. It was enough to make Logan take a step back an pause to take a deep, calming breath. The last thing h needed was to get thrown out of here. Because it wouldn happen. He would get sent to jail for assault before he le without knowing more about Merri's condition.

"She's been looking tired. Pale," Angel offered, clutch ing his black-and-gold New Orleans Saints cap in his hands

A wave of guilt struck Logan. "I know." He'd chosen t ignore it. He'd been feeling miserable himself, and workin like a dog. Wallowing in self-pity, he'd wanted her to fe just as bad.

"It might just be exhaustion," Angel said, with a tenta tive smile that showed his gold front tooth. "Er, should call Miss Faith? My other waitress said that Merri woul want—"

"No one calls my mother until I know what we're deal ing with." Logan knew his mother was probably not home but at Stan Shirley's house until it was time to pick u Danny from school and then Merri; however, he didn't wan to take any chances. At any rate, she had to be contacte soon, or else she would be waiting outside the café, an someone would fill her in whether he wanted them to or not

He tried to think, to plan. There was Danny to protect too.

"Logan? Thank God!"

The sound of his mother's voice sent his insides lurch ing. He wheeled around. "How on earth—?"

"Mike LeBlanc heard about the 911 call on the police ra dio. He called me at Stan's. What's happened to her?"

"We're waiting for news. All we know is that she fainted at work."

Angel stepped toward Faith. "We called for an ambulance right away, Mrs. Powers."

Logan led his mother to a chrome-and-plastic chair, grateful that there were no other people around who were waiting for news on friends or family. The place was institutionally impersonal enough without their having to deal with strangers.

"What about Danny?" he asked her, forcing himself to keep his mind working logically.

"Mike said he would pick him up. Such a kind gesture. He's a good man. Why is it that all the bad things happen to good people?"

Not liking the tone of his mother's voice, Logan redirected her thoughts by pointing out, "Danny will know something's wrong."

"But Mike's trained for this sort of thing."

Next she would be encouraging Meredith to go out with the guy. As an image of Merri and LeBlanc double-dating with her and Stan flashed before his eyes, Logan scowled and returned to his pacing. He was vaguely aware of Angel settling down beside his mother. The two began discussing how they'd both been noticing Merri's frail appearance, how they both felt guilty for not doing more sooner. He told himself he would be damned if he joined in the verbal self-chastisement. Meredith was an adult, responsible for her own body. But that line of thinking soon had him feeling worse.

A nurse came around the corner and eyed them tentatively. Her gaze settled on him. "Mr. Powers?"

"Yes."

"Would you come this way, please? You can see her now."

"May I come, too?" Faith asked, rising. "I'm her mother-in-law."

"I imagine that will be all right."

They followed the nurse to a small room where Merri lay so still Logan thought she must be asleep. She looked very young, and totally drained. He had to fight back the urge to rush to her side. It was his mother who did that and took hold of her hand.

"Dear? It's Faith. Logan's here, too. Can you hear me? You gave us quite a scare, but you're going to be all right."

Merri's blue-veined eyelids lifted slowly, and she stared at her, then beyond her, to where he stood at the foot of the bed. The momentary flash of pleasure in her eyes nearly had him rounding to the other side of the bed and reaching for her other hand.

"Ah! Good, you're here." A smiling young doctor who barely looked old enough to spell *intern* let alone practice medicine, came briskly into the room. "Mr. Powers, is it?"

"Yes," Logan replied automatically. Then he realized what conclusion the man might draw. "That is—"

"I'm Merri's mother-in-law, Faith, Doctor."

"And I'm her brother-in-law," Logan said, wanting the clarification made known before things got more embarrassing.

"Oh. I naturally thought... Um, in any case, I'm happy to report that congratulations are in order."

"You mean she can go home?" Logan asked, his spirits lifting as the younger man's smile returned.

"That, too. But what I meant, Mr. Powers, was that you're going to be an uncle."

A half hour later, as Merri sat in Logan's truck, she continued to shake from shock. *Pregnant?* It just couldn't be true. But it was.

And Logan was furious.

He sat beside her, gripping the steering wheel in a stranglehold. It wouldn't surprise her in the least if he managed to snap it in two; in fact, she almost wished he would. Then the truck would be undrivable. If she couldn't get home, she wouldn't have to face Faith again.

Or Danny.

Dear heaven, how was she going to explain this to Danny?

Her mind worked sluggishly, and in abstract, dizzying leaps back and forth, so that for once she actually welcomed Logan's silence. He hadn't said a word since his mother's gasp back at the hospital. Muttering, "We'll talk about this at the house," he'd stalked out of the room to take care of getting her released. She doubted the condition would last for long once they arrived at the house.

She didn't know if she was up to having three people going at her at one time. The doctor had only released her on the condition that she would climb into bed immediately upon arriving home, but would they care?

Home . . . She groaned silently. There was another potential powder keg. Under the circumstances, did she still have a home?

"Maybe you'd better get in your yelling now," she said, slumping against the headrest and closing her eyes. "This way I'll have one of you down and only two more to deal with when we get to the house."

When the seconds ticked by to almost a half minute, Merri resigned herself to the idea that it would have to be a three-against-one scenario, after all. Too bad the doctor couldn't have prescribed something for her that would allow her to pass out and sleep through the massacre.

"I thought you said it was impossible."

For a moment, she thought she'd imagined his voice. Rolling her head to the left, she gazed at his grim-faced profile. "It is impossible. Was. *Is.*"

"Well, you're obviously wrong."

Thank you, Dr. Einstein.

Regardless of how hard she tried, Merri couldn't accept the reality of the matter. She wanted him to understand that. "First thing tomorrow, I'm going to call for an appointment to have the tests redone. It's all a mistake." It had to be.

"You've been getting run-down for weeks."

How nice of him to finally notice. "So I need a few vitamins."

"That's like saying a totaled car needs a little bodywork."

"The sarcasm is unnecessary, Logan."

"Excuse me all to hell, but I'm a little shaken, all right?" he snapped, briefly taking his eyes off the road to glare at her. "I'm forty-five years old, and single. Less than thirty minutes ago I found out despite all that I'm going to be a father!"

"An uncle."

He shot her a lethal look.

"Well, think about how I feel!"

"I haven't gotten that far yet. Good grief, Meredith, I'm still trying to figure out how you failed to notice you hadn't gone through your regular cycle!"

"For the simple reason that I haven't had a regular *cycle* since the day I started menstruating!"

That seemed to reach him. His hands moved restlessly on the steering wheel and several emotions worked over his face. "Does that constitute a serious problem?"

"Probably not. The doctor I had with Danny said it might have been a result of my nutritional gaps while growing up.

Look, the point is, I'm sorry for not guessing. I'm sorry for getting pregnant.''

"Well...it's not as if you did it on your own," he replied, although he sounded as if the admission had been dragged out of him.

It wasn't much, but it helped Meredith hold on to her control until they arrived at the house. But as she eased out of the truck and approached the back door, she hesitated.

Suddenly Logan cupped a hand under her elbow. "Are you feeling faint again?"

"No. I'm trying to build up some courage. It seems I'm suddenly finding myself in short supply."

"As I said," he replied gruffly, "you didn't do this alone. You don't have to face what's inside alone, either."

She didn't know how many more shocks she could take. "I think I do need to sit down now."

"Yeah, well, I can understand that. But wait until you get inside, all right? And try to stop looking as if I've never done a nice thing in my life."

"Not to me, you haven't."

"Oh, really?"

His voice alone made her rethink that, and when she saw his arched eyebrow, and the blatant sexuality in his look, she felt a totally different kind of dizziness. "Do you mind?" she murmured under her breath as she reached for the doorknob. "*That's* what got us into this mess in the first place."

As she feared, Faith and Danny were waiting for them when they entered. Although her mother-in-law refused to even meet her gaze, Danny rushed over to offer a hug.

"Jeez, Mom, you look awful."

"Thanks. I can't tell you how much I needed to hear that."

"Are you all right? What happened? Gran wouldn't tell me anything except that you fainted at work and needed to rest."

She wanted to cry. No, she wanted to take back that reckless weekend. Oh, but that wasn't true, either. She didn't know what she wanted, except not to have to do this to her son.

"I need to tell you something," she began, giving him a wobbly smile. "And I wish...I wish... Never mind."

"Mom, c'mon... You know you can tell me anything. We've always stuck together no matter what, haven't we?"

She couldn't swallow the boulder in her throat. "Mmm...but this is a whopper. I'm going to have a baby."

His eyes went wide and round. His gaze dropped to her abdomen. "You can't be. You'd have to be big by now."

She couldn't do this. The words were in her head and in her heart, but they refused to come out.

"The baby's mine, Dan."

Merri had felt Logan move closer. She'd thought maybe she looked ready to drop again and he just wanted to be able to catch her in time. Instead, he stepped beside her, suggesting a different message entirely.

Her son swallowed. "This is a joke, right?"

Merri shook her head slowly, and that had Danny stiffening all the more. His jaw worked as he struggled with emotions she could only imagine.

She reached a hand toward him, having never felt more exposed and ineffective. "I'm sorry to upset you."

"Upset? Upset? How am I going to face the kids at school? I'll be a laughingstock."

"You will not. I doubt any of your classmates will pay attention. Rachel has grown since my childhood. Not as many people remember me as I thought might."

His face turned beet red. "What are you talking about, Mom? The old-timers, the new-timers, they're all gonna notice you getting as big as a house!"

"Don't get rude to your mother, Dan."

Merri wasn't the only one who was surprised that Logan had defended her. Danny and Faith were, too. But it was her son who reacted.

"Don't tell me what I can and can't do!" he shouted back. "You're not my father, and you never will be!"

He raced out of the room and up the stairs. Merri ached to go after him, but she knew now wasn't the time. He was angry and disillusioned. When the slam of his bedroom door echoed down to the kitchen, Merri felt her knees buckle and quickly grabbed a chair to sit down.

"Your turn next," Logan said to his mother.

"I don't think I have words to describe all that I'm feeling."

But when she crossed her arms and glared at them, Logan replied, "You'll force yourself to try, though."

"Logan, please." Wishing she could run away, too, Merri buried her face in her hands. "Your mother's hurt. She has a right—"

"Hurt? I'm insulted," Faith snapped. "You betrayed my trust."

That one confused her. "How?"

"You're Brett's wife!"

"Was. And now I'm his widow. I loved him, Faith," Merri said gently. "But I'm not about to crawl into his grave with him."

"That's more than obvious."

Did Faith think that just because she'd decided to stay alone all these years, all Powers women should become social nuns? "I'll admit I'm upset about the pregnancy for any number of reasons, Faith. But I won't comment, let alone apologize for my relationship with Logan."

"What relationship? Most of the time you two find it a chore to say two civil words to each other."

"That's why this is so difficult."

Faith's expression clearly let it be known that she had a problem believing that. "I suppose I know when this happened? And to think I worried about you, felt guilty for leaving you two alone. What I should have done is hired a chaperon. *Teenagers* get into less trouble!"

"That's enough, Mother." Logan went to the refrigerator and took out a beer for himself.

"I don't think I've ever been more disappointed in anyone's behavior in my life."

Logan lifted his eyebrows. "Really? Despite having had a draft-dodger son, who didn't have the courtesy to tell you goodbye before he ran off to Canada? Thank you very much. It's always good to know where one stands in the family." Saluting her with the can, he took a long drink.

Faith drew herself erect. "That's in the past."

"And what's done is done. Isn't that the argument you always used whenever Brett dropped the ball or let someone down? Mother, you know I will always be here for you, but sometimes your double standards wear damned thin."

"Don't talk to me about standards. What I want to know is, what now? Will I have to deal with the knowledge of an abortion, too?"

"No!" Merri leapt to her feat, horrified. "The idea never crossed my mind." She quickly turned to Logan, wanting him to understand that above all.

"At least that's something," Faith said, her voice losing a touch of its frigidity. "Small comfort though it is."

"Then let me add some," Logan said conversationally, as he traced his index finger around the rim of his can. "I intend to do right by Meredith."

Merri's heart gave a frantic jolt at the old-fashioned phrasing. *"What?"*

"I'm going to marry you."

Logan waited outside the bathroom for a full three minutes before he tapped lightly. "Just tell me if you're conscious...."

"Go away."

"I'm coming in."

He eased the door open, not knowing whether to expect a scream or a scrub brush across the nose. What he found was Merri sitting on the side of the bathtub, her face buried in a damp washcloth.

"Feeling sick again?"

"Dizzy."

"Let me rinse that cloth for you and cool it off," he said, taking it from her. He held it under the faucet and soaked it with cold well water. Once he'd wrung most of the excess liquid out, he pressed it back into her hands. "Here. Is that better?"

"Stop shocking me, Logan. I've had all I can deal with for one day."

"I'm only trying to help. Maybe I haven't given you a cause to believe that before, but it's true."

"You think proposing marriage is help? Your mother was right—we can barely be in a room together for ten minutes before the atmosphere begins to disintegrate. Do you think I want to bring my child into that kind of environment?"

"*Our* child. And we'll change."

She glanced up, her expression droll. "As easy as that, huh?"

This woman was carrying his child. He'd resigned himself to the idea that having a wife and children simply wasn't in the cards for him. Now that it had happened, however it had happened, did she think he was going to let the opportunity, let *her*, slip through his fingers?

"We can try."

"You're giving me that look again," she muttered, ducking behind the terry cloth.

"You may have to get used to it."

Merri groaned. "This isn't necessary, Logan. There's always the possibility that I won't be able to carry the baby to term. Between my age and my medical history, it's a strong possibility. Why tie yourself to a marriage for a situation that could change at any time?"

Although the possibility wasn't a complete surprise, considering what she'd told him before, Logan had to deal with a surge of panic. "Don't even think that. From here on out, you're going to start thinking positive, understood?"

"Oh, great. My husband, the frustrated coach." As soon as she saw him begin to smile, she blurted out hastily, "That was just an expression! No, Logan, forget it. It isn't going to happen."

As she rose and brushed past him, he followed. When she entered her room and tried to shut the door, he easily forced his way in.

Looking definitely hunted, Merri pleaded, "I need to lie down. If I don't get some peace and quiet—"

Without bothering to reply or argue, Logan swept her into his arms and carried her the few feet to the full-size bed that had been Brett's. Then he sat down beside her. "Better?"

"It would be if you'd go away."

"I will as soon as we come to an agreement." His gaze was drawn by the photo of Brett on the night table. He didn't want to deal with the myriad emotions and memories the picture spawned, and without comment he set it inside the table's top drawer. "You're going to marry me, Meredith," he continued quietly.

"What if I decided to run away instead?"

He shook his head, pleased with the calmness he felt. "Your running days are over. Besides, you wouldn't do that to Dan...or the baby. I may not always understand you, but I'm beginning to read you rather well."

As he took the cloth, folded it and placed it neatly across her head, he added, "I'll take care of you, all of you. You won't want for anything."

"But we're not in love!"

His gaze shifted to her hands. She was unconsciously twisting her wedding band. It gave him great pleasure to gently but firmly take hold of her and slip the thing off. He put it in with the photograph, murmuring, "We'll get you a new ring tomorrow."

"I have to work."

"Wrong."

"Logan!"

"Tomorrow." He leaned over her, bracing his hands on either side of her. "We're good in bed. That's more than many people have. I want the baby, Meredith...and I want you. Give it a chance."

Eight

The wedding was hardly a celebration. Logan made all the arrangements, and exactly ten days later managed to get his family to stop sulking long enough that he and Merri could exchange their vows. He hadn't worked so hard since his second year in business, when a hurricane had ripped half the roof off a house he was supposed to have ready for closing. As it was, he barely succeeded in getting the bride to show up.

Right after her initial doctor's appointment, which he attended with her, he'd made it clear that she would follow the doctor's advice and not work her full shift at the café. The hours on her feet and the demands of the job could add to potential complications. But Merri—how easy it was getting for him to think of her as Merri now—had refused to leave Angel in a bind. She'd worked until the end of September—yesterday, to be exact—when she knew that she'd been adequately replaced.

Logan had even bought her a dress for today. As he watched her standing with Sherman, who'd served as one of their witnesses, and the minister, he felt rather pleased with himself at the results. The pale blue crepe sheath had been in the window of an Alexandria store. He'd been up there checking out a potential new fixture supplier, and he'd spotted it while stopping for a traffic light. On impulse, he'd stopped to see if they carried the dress in a size four, having discovered her size by snooping in her closet one day, when no one else had been around. The necessity of doing that still rankled, but he knew that if he hadn't, she would have shown up today in her jeans and one of those blasted peasant shirts.

Instead, she looked as if she'd slid down a moonbeam. Maybe she had a point about the chiffon sleeves being a bit much for such a small, brief service; but to him she'd never looked more feminine or romantic. "You're determined to turn me into a traditionalist, aren't you?" she'd asked with a grimace. But he'd caught her eyeing herself in a mirror several times already.

As if she felt his gaze, she looked through the doorway of the kitchen to where he stood in the living room. He'd had to take a call from his one of his foremen. The calls couldn't be helped, since he'd stayed home all day to make sure his bride, as well as Dan and his mother, didn't try anything to delay the service.

From the faint pink flush in Merri's cheeks, he knew she was embarrassed at being caught admiring the small spray of blue daisies, white freesia and baby's breath he'd had made for her. They were the closest thing to wildflowers the florist could come up with at this time of year. All Logan thought was that they suited her more than roses or carnations, because the little rebel was his wildflower girl, whether she wanted to be or not.

My wife. Logan drew in a deep breath, feeling a quiet satisfaction. Mutinous though she was, rebellious and irreverent, she was his now. Tonight she would sleep in his bed.

For the first time in his life, he felt a hint of what happiness could be. The affection and good intentions he'd felt for Jane didn't compare. This was closer to the real thing, wasn't it? Maybe they had both nearly choked over the reference to love while exchanging their vows, maybe they still argued at the slightest shift in the barometer, but there was something basic and compelling between them. And he'd eat his damned tie if it was only sex.

What do you feel? he asked with his gaze.

She hastily shifted her attention back to the minister and Sherman, who were finally taking their leave. So be it, Logan thought. For now. She could act as if she were being forced into doing something against her will, but he would teach her to accept his possessiveness, just as he intended to teach her that she could enjoy being a little dependent, too. They were a unit now, a team. No, a partnership. Good things could come from that. His family had existed with too many handicaps for too long. So had hers. He didn't like what they'd all grown to accept as "normal." He would create a healthy, loving home by the sheer force of his willpower, if he had to. They needed this, all of them, even if they were too stubborn to admit it yet.

Setting the phone down, he returned to the kitchen. His mother was covering a sliced ham with plastic wrap. He reached beneath quickly before she tucked the ends under, and snatched another piece.

"I'm glad someone around here has an appetite," she muttered, briskly continuing with the chore. "I told you it wasn't necessary to prepare so much food."

"A ham, a little potato salad and a small cake isn't too much food. Besides, I noticed Sherman was happy to take a platter with him." While he understood her lingering coolness toward them, he wouldn't let her ruin his mood. "Did Dan eat anything before he left for Larry's?"

"What do you think? As soon as he could, he ran upstairs to change and raced out of here."

The I-told-you-so tone got under his skin a bit, and he had to pause a moment before murmuring, "If this becomes a totally intolerable situation, Mother, say the word. We can always move out." In fact, he had a recently completed house that hadn't yet sold; the folks who'd originally contracted it hadn't been able to sell their place. He knew Merri would hate the prestigious, ornate dwelling, but as a temporary residence...

"Don't be ridiculous. And what am I supposed to do in this huge place by myself?"

"I would worry over you, too." Swallowing the last of the ham, he quickly bent to kiss her cheek. "So please stop trying to punish us."

Without waiting for her to respond, he went to his bride, who'd just shut the door after their departing guests. Boxing her against it, he smiled down at her. "Okay?"

Her answering look held a mild rebuke. "You know Reverend Hale is taking you seriously. He expects us to start attending services. Regularly."

"Do you have a problem with that?"

"I guess not. But I'm drawing the line at joining the ladies' group he mentioned."

"Too 'traditional' for you?" Logan teased, wanting badly to kiss her until she clung to him.

"Too gossipy. We have...*had* several groups who regularly came into Angel's. The day I sense I'm turning into one of those holier-than-thou biddies, I'm going straight out and getting a tattoo.''

Logan pursed his lips. ''Hmm...do I get to choose where it goes?''

''Stop laughing at me.''

''Can't. You're cute when you stick your nose in the air.''

''I'm too old to be cute.'' But her indignant expression quickly gave way to one of dismay. ''Oh, Logan...what are we doing?''

Touched by her sincerity, he stroked her cheek. ''Making the best of things. Life goes on, Merri. Remember?''

''I saw Danny leave.''

''It's not as if we don't know where he is. He'll be back.''

''Your mother didn't even hug me after the service,'' she continued, dropping her voice to a whisper.

''You want a hug? Come here.'' Slipping his arms around her, he gently drew her against him. It wasn't the best fit. He would have preferred lifting her until they fit the way he liked, but it was a sweet beginning.

''You're very patient with me.''

''I know you're trying, too.''

''I *do* love the flowers. I know I didn't thank you before, but they're exactly what I would have chosen myself.''

''I know that, too.''

She leaned back to gaze up at him. ''Why haven't you ever let me see this side of you before?''

Before she hadn't been around. Before that, they'd been too young. Patience, tolerance, *bending,* came with time, experience and maturity—and even then not everyone learned their lessons. But this was hardly the time to get philosophical. Instead, he murmured, ''You've never been carrying my baby before.'' She'd never worn his ring on her finger before.

Their gazes clung. Logan saw an invitation in the deep pools of her eyes that stoked a fire in the pit of his belly and inched a groan up his throat. God, yes, he wanted to kiss her to make up for that sterile little peck they'd exchanged after the ceremony. But he knew that if he began, he would want to finish properly, and no doubt his mother was already noticing how long they'd been back here.

"Why don't you go upstairs and move your things into my room?" he suggested gruffly. They'd already discussed that, and gotten Faith's reluctant permission to turn Brett's old room into a nursery. "I'll be up to help you as soon as I make a few more calls. I made room for you everywhere, but if you need more..."

"Oh, stop. You know darned well you're the first man since Uglug the Neanderthal to acquire a wife who could put all her worldly possessions into one bag." Playfully tapping her bouquet against his chest, she eased out of his arms and slipped past him.

"Meredith, would you like to put those flowers in water so you can take them up to your room?"

Logan thought it ironic that he and his mother had completely reversed what they called her, but he was grateful she'd bent enough to offer the suggestion. He exchanged glances with his bride.

"Yes, that sounds like a lovely idea." When Faith took a slender crystal vase from a cabinet, Merri thanked her again, filled it with water and added the flowers.

Watching her go upstairs, Logan knew he'd never seen her look lovelier. He wouldn't be able to wait until tonight to be with her. The need to hold her in his arms and absorb the reality of their union was too strong.

"My God." His mother's whisper sounded as humble as it did surprised. "It's not just...the physical thing, is it?"

He tucked his hands into his pants pockets and simply smiled at his mother.

"Do you mind me asking . . . how long?"

He shrugged. "Who can say?"

She seemed to need a moment to chew over that. Finally she crossed to him and embraced him. "I'm sorry for being an old prude. I've had to adapt so often to sudden changes over the years, I think I put on the brakes at the wrong time."

"No problem." How could he hold a grudge? She was an integral part of his dream for his family. "Thanks for all the work you did, and for giving up your time with Stan."

"He doesn't dislike you, you know. He knows Jane's found her happiness. He's simply unsure how to act toward you. Sometimes you can be standoffish, you know."

"So I've been told recently, although not quite in those words." He cast another glance toward the stairs. "And what about you? Are you going to let Stan make *you* happy?"

"It's different when you're my age. But I won't say I'm not tempted," she admitted, looking bemused.

"That's good. If you can't take giant steps, take baby steps." She'd been inching back from life for too long. They all had. He knew that now.

The house had settled down for the night when Merri left the bathroom and headed for Logan's room—*her* and Logan's room. She could hear the faint sound of Danny's radio playing behind his closed door, and down the hall Faith's TV. Not unlike many a night since she and her son had moved in here, yet different. That was what made all this so strange; everything looked the same, but things were different.

She carefully shut the bedroom door. Logan was already waiting for her, and the butterflies in her stomach fluttered with renewed life as she approached his side of the bed.

"What did you do, reinvent water?"

"Soap."

His lamp was on, and he lay in the center of the king-size walnut bed with his arms crossed beneath his head. *My husband,* she thought, wondering how long it would take to get used to the idea. Maybe when he didn't look quite so much like the conquering hero, triumphant and more than a little pleased with himself.

From the waist up, he was naked, and the light skimmed across the generous plane of his muscular chest and arms, his trim belly. The light enhanced his bronzed skin, and the sheen on the mat of black hair that arrowed beyond the sheet. She thought of how she'd blissfully nuzzled it, combed her fingers through it again and again as she lay exhausted but sated against him during the weekend that had led them to this moment. Her fingers trembled in anticipation of experiencing all that again, and she had difficulty untying the knot.

"Need help?"

"You could turn the light off." Erotic thoughts aside, she was feeling a little vulnerable. His unblinking stare didn't help.

Instead of doing as she asked, Logan rose on his right elbow and loosened the sash himself. She wore nothing beneath the white silk kimono-style robe, and already her insides were humming in anticipation of having his eager, exploring hands on her body again.

"Take it off," he coaxed, his voice a rough murmur.

Yes, regardless of her disbelief that she could find herself married again, and to her true nemesis, no less, she had to admit she wanted this. As she let the robe glide off her shoulders and down her arms, she relished the way his gaze caressed her, the way she felt her body change because of it.

He drew back the sheet, and she slipped beneath it. But he brought the fresh-smelling percale only as far as her hips—in order to splay his hand over her belly, she soon realized. At the moment, he could nearly span the width of her.

"I can't wait until you start showing."

That surprised her. She'd come to believe most men would prefer to forgo that part of a pregnancy. Brett, who'd actually written poetry about her condition and the meaning of fatherhood, had in fact become progressively more remote. Toward the end of her term, he'd avoided intimacy altogether. She didn't want to make comparisons, but as she gazed at the gold band on Logan's ring finger, she knew it would be the height of irony if he surprised her by really meaning what he'd said.

"You don't believe me," he murmured, when she failed to reply.

As he directed his fingers lower, she experienced the delicious quickening inside her and let her eyes drift closed. "I want to."

"Then do."

A great shadow obliterated the light behind her shut lids, and an instant later she felt him cover her mouth with his. Within seconds he had reduced her to a creature of sensation. She welcomed the pressure of his kiss, anticipated the race to fiery passion. But this time there weren't the acute emotions that had driven previous kisses. The man she had thought devoid of tenderness showed her how wrong she could be.

He slanted his lips for better access, and more willing than she had ever been, Merri parted hers. She sighed when he nibbled at her as if she were exotic fruit, licked her as if she vere the source of the rarest honey, stroked her as if he vould never taste her kind again and wanted to capture it ll. And with every stroke or love bite, his gifted hand harted another course of enchantment.

He'd reinvented passion for her, but now he defined true rentleness. Merri had never thought it could be so sensual, et alone so potent. He'd barely begun to trace kisses down er neck, and she knew she was already addicted to them, o him. So much so that she had only to feel his breath on er breasts and she was reaching to draw him down to her, arching to get closer, sooner.

Maybe it was her condition, or maybe it was the man, but he'd become more sensitive there. A few brushes of his lips, trokes of his tongue, the lazy rhythmic suckling that puck-red her nipple to a sweetly painful tautness, and she began o tremble all over. By the time he moved on to her other reast, she was incredibly slick and aching to have him in-side her.

Her restless moves gave away her frustrated state. Nip-ing her waist, Logan murmured, "Easy. Stay with me."

She wanted to—what he did, anything he would do, she new would be wonderful—but when his breath stroked er thigh, she didn't think she could survive it. "Lo-;an ... I'm—"

"I know. But I've been dreaming about being with you again. Let me show you how much."

He did, and in doing so he again taught Merri that no one would ever know her—body or soul—better than he did. The memories of their weekend together would always re-main a vivid image in her mind, but now he engraved a more xquisite one in her heart.

By the time he rose over her and claimed her body with is, she was still quaking from her first climax, and the hot trength of his invasion almost precipitated another. Want-

ing him to know how deeply he'd moved her, she looked u
at him, only to be awed by what she saw. Yes, he was mes
merizing, with his eyes closed tight in ecstasy and concer
tration. But beyond that, she saw beauty radiating fro
inside him, and she knew it was a beauty that only she ha
been able to reach.

The words would have to wait. But she knew tonight wa
indeed, special. Their real beginning.

Tightening her arms, she felt the muscles across his bac
bunch and ripple, his thrusts deepen, but with a restraine
intensity. Once again she realized that the strength of th
external man didn't begin to match the power of the inne
person he'd grown up to become. Eager to have, and t
hold, Merri wrapped her legs around him more tightly, an
let him carry them to a breathtaking mutual release.

One of the most wondrous memories she could remem
ber after their secret weekend had been the way Loga
hadn't abandoned her afterward. An indeterminable tim
later, when he tucked her spoon-fashion against him, sh
uttered a sigh of contentment and gratitude.

"Mmm..." he replied, his warm breath tickling her ea
"Me, too."

"I think you're in serious danger of spoiling me."

"Could I?"

Merri stared at the framed photograph of a bayou land
scape at night and listened to the curiosity—no, wistful
ness—in his question. She bit her lip, wondering, an
decided to take a chance. "How much did your mother te
you about our life after we left here?"

"Very little," he admitted slowly. "You already know
wouldn't let her read me your letters. I even went so far a
to avoid looking at that photograph of you two that's bee
in plain view downstairs since the day it arrived."

"Just as I've tried not to look at yours, or your medals."
Merri shifted onto her back, because she needed to see his
expression. "I think we have a lot to learn about each other
outside of this bed, Logan."

"I want that," he replied, brushing her bangs off her
forehead. "As long as none of it has to do with *him*."

He still felt that way? "I thought..."

"My feelings for you are separate. If you want to talk
about something, I want it to be about you. Us."

"But a major part of who I am is tied up with Brett."

"And that's the part I don't want to hear about. Ever."

That was wrong. Worse, it was impossible. "You can't do
that—make rules and divide a person's life into acceptable
and unacceptable portions."

"It's the only thing I'll ask of you." His own tense state
became as evident as the scar on his chin, showing white
against his tanned and flushed face. "I don't ask you to listen to me talk about the war or Jane, do I?"

"No. But I'd listen now... if you want to..."

"I've put it behind me. There's only today. You. My
business. Our family."

"Logan, I have a son. I owe him the memories of his father."

"Not around *me!*"

Merri's temper rose, too. "You aren't interested in having a wife, you want a mistress who you dictate to, and
control. Someone who doesn't have the right to speak up
when she disagrees with you. Well, no, thank you!"

"Where do you think you're going?" he demanded as she
flung back her side of the sheet.

"I don't know, but—"

Before she could finish, Logan hooked his arm around
her waist and flung her back against the pillows.

"Logan—the baby!"

Realization and shame etched themselves sharply on his hard face as he slowly touched her abdomen. "Oh, God," he whispered, lowering his head until his cheek touched her stomach. "I'm sorry."

She couldn't let him believe it was that easy. "Brett may not have been perfect, although there were many who thought he was, but he never, *never* treated me the way you are now, Logan."

He lifted his head and frowned at her. "Since when did you start thinking he wasn't perfect?"

If she gaped like a fool, it was his doing. "Where have you been? Haven't you been listening to anything I've said over the last several months?"

"Just tell me."

"Oh, now it's okay to talk about him?"

He bowed his head and sighed heavily. "I don't blame you for being disgusted with me."

"What I am is hurt . . . and offended. After you stood up for me in front of your mother, I thought we had a chance at building something solid. But your blind spot toward your brother is going to destroy it before we get started."

"It's not a blind spot, Merri. It's sheer jealousy, laced with years of resentment."

"You?" She wriggled to sit up and secured the sheet under her arms. "How many years?"

"You were there. But not even you saw it—and you saw more than most, for a little kid." Raking back his hair, Logan shifted onto his side. "We used to be close, did you know that?"

"Mmm . . . Brett used to talk about how you would take him fishing and frog-gigging . . . all those things that fathers do with their sons."

"I had to. He was just a runt when Dad died. He looked to me for everything. Eventually my mother did, too."

"You acquired responsibility fast."

"Faster than I should have. Faster than was fair for a kid my age, but I asked for it. I wanted to help my mother. The thing is, I thought Brett would feel the same way, that we'd share responsibility, the way we did everything else."

"He let you down," Merri murmured, sadly.

"Again and again and again."

She looked at a point over his left shoulder, but her view was of years ago. "I used to think it was his sensitivity, his idealistic but beautiful view of life." She smiled wryly. "Whatever I know of the artistic world, he taught me. You have to admit he was bright."

"Oh, yeah. He was that. But people like to forget that it matters what you do with your gifts."

"He used people," Merri said softly, before he could.

Once again Logan looked stunned. "You *knew?*"

"Eventually it sinks in. By then I had a son who he charmed from sunrise to sunset, the way he had me. To be fair, Brett tried to be a good husband. He just wasn't capable of being responsible. Once he knew a person could manage without him, he let them. It simply wasn't in him to be there for you when the chips were down. It was as if he thought his talent exempted him."

Logan's mouth tightened as he nodded. "I tried to warn my mother about that, but all she saw was his cuteness, never the conniving."

"If she had," Merri mused sadly, "he might have learned a bit of stick-to-itiveness. As it was, money stayed a constant problem, because he was always giving up poetry to paint, or giving up painting to write full-time. In between, he did sell some poems to magazines, but when they did pay,

it wasn't much. And when there was a fair of some kind, h
did pastel portraits or charcoal caricatures.'' She shook he
head. ''Then there was the time he got starry-eyed over ar
idea someone gave him about publishing his own collected
poems. We ended up with over a thousand copies from
vanity press, and there wasn't a bookstore within fifty mile
of us. Did your mother show you the copy I sent her?''

''Oh, yes.'' Logan's expression grew hard, his eyes mur
derous. ''So you worked any job you could to survive?''

Merri touched his cheek. ''It was my decision, Logan
Don't forget that. And heaven knows, it was better thar
what I'd had as a kid.'' She pressed her lips to his. ''Thanl
you for finally opening up.''

''You're bad for my discipline, Mrs. Powers. When yo
first came back to Rachel, I was planning to hold a grudg
for at least twenty more minutes.'' As quickly as the smil
came, it dimmed. ''You were always a thought that wouldn'
go away, Merri. But you were so damned young. I wa
hoping that by the time I got out of the service, you woul
have outgrown my brother and been ready for me.''

He was breaking her heart. ''So much time...''

''And we're not out of the woods yet.'' He traced his in
dex finger from her elbow to shoulder and across her col
larbone. ''I think my mother is getting used to the idea. Bu
Dan's a different story. This baby couldn't be worse timing
for him.''

''We'll work it out.''

He looked deeply into her eyes. ''I hope we can. I worr
about the statistics on couples who fail with better odds tha
us, though.''

''But we're not a statistic,'' she reminded him gently
''And who knows? It could be that we have one up on othe

people because we've already made our share of dumb mistakes."

Logan eased her onto her back and framed her face with his hands. "Lady, lady...I could get a little crazy over you."

"I'm willing."

Nine

"**I** hate like hell having to leave you today," Logan tol
Merri as she walked him to his truck. "But people are wait
ing to close on the Royal Lane house, and if I put them o
until Monday, they'll have to pay a weekend's storage fee t
the moving company. They're out-of-staters with no plac
to set everything."

"I understand," Merri insisted, although it made her fee
warm inside that he'd only explained the situation thre
times already.

"Are you sure you're going to be all right? Unless some
thing goes awry, I should be done by early afternoon."

"That's fine. *I'll* be fine. Maybe I'll use the time to star
working on the new nursery. Drawing that sketch yo
wanted. Maybe make some lists. Box things away."

"Great, but hey—no moving anything heavy," Loga
warned. "Promise?"

"Wouldn't think of it." Patting her stomach, she beamed up at him. "Now get going, will you? The sooner you leave, the sooner you'll be back."

"Hold that thought."

Logan drew her into his arms for another long kiss. It drew a soft moan of desire from her, as it stirred memories of the achingly sweet passion they'd rediscovered after their soul-wrenching talk last night. Before Logan lifted his head again, Merri felt as weak as a baby and had to cling to him to stay on her feet.

"Now maybe you'll miss me," he murmured against her lips.

"Are you kidding? After a kiss like that, a woman would be doing well to remember her own name."

Laughing softly, Logan kissed her on the forehead and finally climbed into the truck. Merri stayed outside to wave him off until he disappeared down the road. A bemused but satisfied smile continued to linger, even as she went back into the house.

Faith was at the stove, making Danny's breakfast—a routine she'd insisted on initiating shortly after they moved in—but he hadn't yet come downstairs. Her mother-in-law had been pleasant enough when she and Logan came downstairs, but Merri couldn't help but wonder how they would get along when alone.

"Maybe you should eat something, too," Faith said, glancing over her shoulder. "I know you don't usually care for breakfast, but you remember what the doctor said about maintaining your strength through more than vitamins."

"Sure do, but it's a little early for me to look at food. I'll start with a glass of milk."

"Good. What are your plans for today? The reason I'm asking is that Stan is going to get his cast off this morning, and I've volunteered to take him. Of course, if you needed the car, I suppose Mike could—"

"No, no! By all means, keep with your schedule. You don't worry about me. I'm going to behave like the doctor ordered, and play the lady of leisure."

Faith's answering look exposed her amused skepticism. "That'll be the day."

Grateful for the hint of friendship returning in her mother-in-law's tone, Merri grinned. "Well, I'll try anyway." Pouring herself the milk, she took her seat again. "I meant to tell you, I saw Mike the other day. He was having lunch with Terri Brooks."

"Hmm...Terri Brooks. Now how do I know that name?"

"She's opening the new day-care center on Pecan Avenue."

"Oh, yes. I met her at the grocery store. She was filling up her basket with pumpkins, and I couldn't help but ask her what she was going to do with them all. She's a pretty thing."

"Sweet-natured, too, from what I hear. One of the waitresses at Angel's had a meeting with her because she wants to sign up her little girl. I think Mike may have found someone special in her."

"I can't wait to tell Stan," Faith replied, sounding relieved. "He loves Mike like his own son, and— Well, good morning, dear!"

Danny shuffled into the room, his shoulders slumped and his eyes still puffy from sleeping. He murmured a low greeting without looking at either of them, and announced that Larry's mother would be driving them both to school this morning.

"Fine." But Merri continued to observe her son, wondering when he'd shut off that radio last night. She made a mental note to keep an eye on that. "What do you want to drink with breakfast? Milk? Juice?"

"Nothing. I don't want anything to eat, either."

"But, Danny, dear," Faith said, "you have to have something. It's such a long time before lunch."

"I don't care."

"Don't be rude to your grandmother," Merri warned him quietly. "If you're angry at me, that's one thing, but don't take it out on an innocent party."

His sidelong look held unmistakable resentment. "I wasn't rude. I just don't care, okay! No one else around here cares, so why should I?"

As he slammed out of the house, Merri stared. Shaking her head, she gestured to a somber-faced Faith. "I apologize. That is not my son. I don't know who that person was who just stormed out of here, but he was not the boy I raised."

"This is a tough time for him, dear. He'll adjust."

But even after Faith left for Stan's, Merri brooded over that awful scene. The one thing she'd taken comfort in was that she'd never had to worry about her relationship with her son. They'd always had a unique closeness and honesty. Of course, her relationship with Logan and her pregnancy would have caused some challenge for him, but considering their history, why hadn't he at least tried to give her the benefit of the doubt? Where had this tendency to hastily jump to conclusions come from?

At least he had a friend now with whom he could vent his feelings, Merri thought. As for her, she needed to keep busy, or else this negative start to the day would turn into depression. She didn't want to greet Logan with a long face.

After making up their bed and straightening the room, Merri stepped across the hallway and opened the door to her former bedroom. Brett's old room.

She sighed. "It's time to get on with the job of living Brett."

He would always be a part of this family, their lives. She would always be glad he'd given her Danny. No matter how he'd failed or disappointed people or himself in life, he could be proud of that accomplishment. But she wouldn't build a shrine around his memory, for Danny's sake or any one else's, and this room couldn't remain one, either. The family couldn't heal or grow that way.

The nursery will bring an aura of fresh air into the place, she thought, going downstairs for the boxes Faith had told her were stored in the utility area. The thought of the miracle growing inside her helped buoy her hopefulness. A new life would keep everyone in the house young. "Whether we're ready or not," she added with a chuckle.

An hour later, she sat on the edge of the bed and looked around the room. Except for the furniture itself, everything was packed into the four big boxes she'd brought upstairs. All that remained was Brett's framed photograph, which had been on the bedside table and now lay on her lap.

She wouldn't pack this away. Her instinct was to give it to Danny. Maybe not today or tomorrow, but later. He could have it in his room. Maybe once he saw that he didn't have to hide the existence of his father, that she wasn't asking that of him, he would feel more secure about the rest.

"What are you doing?"

Lost in thought, she hadn't heard anyone come in. Barely stifling a gasp, Merri pressed a hand to her heart and swung around to see Danny in the doorway.

"You scared me to death! And what are you doing home? You're supposed to be in school."

"I didn't go."

Dread was like a lead weight crushing her happiness. "You cut class?" He'd never acted so irresponsibly before! "Danny, that's not good."

"I asked you what you're doing with that? With this room?" He ventured closer to examine each box. As he moved from one to the other, his young face grew more taut, more an angry red. "You're getting rid of him."

"No, honey! That's not it at all."

"You're throwing him away because you have someone else to take his place. What's next to get tossed out? Me?"

"Danny!"

"That's why you got pregnant, isn't it? You and Logan plan to pay Dad back for what he thinks Dad did to him. I've figured it out from listening to you guys when you thought I wasn't. Gran liked Dad better than Logan, and so Logan's going to pay Dad back by replacing me with his kid!"

It was the most outrageous idea she'd ever heard. But Merri knew better than to tell her son his logic was unsound. With his self-esteem already bruised, that would only make matters worse.

Feeling totally out of her depth and unqualified, she rose and held out the photo to him. "We're not going to forget your father, Danny. In fact, I was just looking at this picture of him that I took shortly after you were born. I thought you would like to have it in your room."

He took it from her and held it close to his chest. "One thing's for certain, you don't deserve to have it."

"That will be enough," Merri demanded, fighting to keep the pain from her voice. "I want to sympathize with you for what you're going through, but I will not let you talk to me or anyone else in that fashion."

"You have no right to lecture me. Look at you—you're the one who got *pregnant* without being married. Dad's not even gone six months yet! You know, when I was a kid, I once heard someone whisper about Dad being a coward and a traitor to his country, but at least he was honest about what he believed in and felt. You—you're nothing but a hypocrite!''

He rushed from the room, leaving Merri bent over at the waist, feeling as if he'd ripped out her heart. Too hurt to cry, she stumbled after him. ''Danny! Danny, wait a minute! *Danny!*''

The only answer she received was the resounding slam of the back door.

Feeling sick to her stomach, she sank down at the top of the stairs and gripped the corner post. Her heart was racing like an overworked steam engine, and she was close to hyperventilating.

Calm down, she told herself. The worst thing she could do was panic. Although her instinct was to chase after her son, she knew she had to think of the baby more than herself. Danny would feel better after he had time to cool off. Being a teenager was tough enough, without the stress they'd all been dealing with lately. All parents went through a few rough moments with their kids.

But, dear Lord, it hurt.

If she could lie down for a few minutes, the pain would ease, and the panic, too. She would be rested and ready when Danny came back to talk out the situation.

Although shaky, she pushed herself to her feet and retreated to her and Logan's bed. There she curled up into a tight ball and closed her eyes.

Logan whistled as he killed the truck's engine. His schedule hadn't been improvable, but at least he hadn't returned home later than he'd hoped. It was barely past two when he entered the house and called, ''I'm home!''

The fact that his mother's station wagon wasn't parked outside didn't disappoint him, but that was because he was hoping Merri hadn't gone somewhere with her. Unless... He glanced at his watch again and nodded in realization.

School was just getting out. Maybe the two of them had gone to pick up Dan.

Deciding that would give him myers for a quick shower, he resumed his humming and took the stairs two at a time. At the top, he began tugging loose his tie. A smile tugged at his lips, as it had on and off all day, whenever he thought of Merri. It died the moment he saw her on the bed.

"Sweetheart—?" Her position alone had the hairs on the back of his neck rising. When he saw how pale she was, and her tear-marked face, he sat down on the edge of the bed, his heart beginning to thud. "Merri," he coaxed, touching her forehead. She was burning up.

His cool touch roused her. Blinking, she focused on him, and with an incoherent whisper she sat up to wrap her arms tightly around him.

"I'm so glad you're back. I didn't know what to do. Is he home yet? He didn't mean it, I know, but it hurt so much."

"Whoa..." Although her reaching out to him thrilled him, Logan couldn't understand exactly what she was talking about. "What's happened? Who didn't mean what? No, first things first. Are you sick? You're running another fever."

"I'm okay. Tired. I did feel queasy, but I thought if I lay down for a while it would go away."

"Has it?"

"Not really. It's Danny, Logan. Is he home yet?"

"Not that I know of. Why? What did he do?"

She proceeded to tell him about what had happened after he left. It was upsetting enough to hear how hard she'd worked in Brett's old bedroom; when she related her confrontation with Danny, he grew furious.

"That little—"

"No, Logan! We've been so caught up in each other, I haven't given him the attention he needed. You didn't see how upset he was."

"But he was out of line to say what he did to you." Logan hugged her tighter, wishing he'd been here for her, to spare her this. "Why didn't you call me?"

"I didn't want you to worry about me or have to deal with this."

"Your problems are my problems, sweetheart." What was more, he was determined to have her thinking clearly about Danny's behavior. "Look, if you'd been negligent, or careless with him in the past, that would be one thing, but it isn't. This is jealousy, and a play for power, and he's not going to get away with it."

"I think he already has. Oh, Logan, the worst part is that I don't know where he is. I can only hope he made it to school, but he obviously missed his ride with Larry this morning."

"Listen to you," Logan said, stroking her hair and trying to sound as if she were making much out of something trivial. Inside, however, he felt torn between wanting to shake some sense into the kid and carrying Merri to a doctor for a checkup. "If it will make you feel better, I'll go check with Sherman and find out if he's seen or heard anything. By then Mom should be home with him. If he's not with her, I'll take a drive to the school to look around."

"If you give me a second to splash water on my face, I'll come with you."

He would have none of that. "You stay right here. If he phones, someone has to take the call."

"I hadn't thought of that."

Glad he'd made her see reason, Logan kissed her again. After coaxing her to keep trying to rest until his return, he went in search of his stepson.

He met Faith outside. One look at her face, and he knew she'd come from the school and hadn't seen the boy. He quickly filled her in on what Merri had told him. "I'm going to talk to Sherman, and then I'll swing over to the Brendans. After that, the school. I'll be in touch by my car phone."

"Is Merri cramping or anything?" Faith called after him, more concerned now than when she'd arrived.

"She's running a fever, and I know she's been crying, but I don't think the baby is giving her problems. Thanks, Mom."

Despite feeling better about leaving Merri, Logan's spirits took a dive when Sherman failed to give him the information he'd been hoping for. As a result, his trip to the Brendan home was made with growing concern.

Larry Brendan was, indeed, home, and he and his mother were courteous, although Larry looked a bit uncomfortable at being questioned. Mrs. Brendan noticed that, and firmly urged Larry to tell what he knew, until he admitted that Dan had been deeply upset over his mother's wedding.

"Do you have any idea where he would go if he didn't come here?" Logan asked, watching the boy's expression carefully for any sign of evasion or deceit.

"No, sir. Honest. If you'd asked me that yesterday, I'd have said he would come here, but now..." The boy shrugged.

Thanking them, and asking them to call the house if they saw or heard anything, Logan continued on his way. But where else to look? he wondered.

For the next few hours, he checked out the cemetery, the ball parks in the area, downtown, and the school again—all without success. Reluctantly he phoned the house to report the bad news. While not surprised, Merri was understandably upset.

"I'm going to call the police," she announced, her voice breaking.

As much as he agreed in theory, Logan knew he had to caution her. "They won't file a missing-persons report for twenty-four hours, sweetheart."

"Well, at least they could be made aware of the situation."

"You're right. Do you want me to call?"

"No. I'll do it. Will you keep looking?"

"You know I will."

Merri's call to the police and sheriff's departments produced some effect. By dusk Logan had been stopped several times by law enforcement people who assured him they would be doing all they could to help; however, when another hour passed and no one contacted him, he knew he needed to go home for the night, be with Merri. His heart heavy, he made a U-turn and headed back toward town.

About to turn off onto his farm-to-market road, he was flashed by an oncoming vehicle, which then turned its overhead lights on. It was Mike LeBlanc, he realized moments later, when the officer pulled over and crossed the road to talk to him. Belatedly Logan saw the passenger door open and a smaller person emerge.

"Dan?"

"I found him sleeping in a church on the road to Melville," LeBlanc told him. "Somebody'd reported seeing lights and thought the place was being vandalized."

"I appreciate it," Logan said, difficult as it was to be beholden to the man he'd recently been so jealous of. "Will there be any charges pressed, do you think?"

"Nah. I already talked to the minister there. All he wanted was reassurance that Dan would be taken care of and his family problems resolved."

"We definitely hope to do that."

After politely inviting the deputy sheriff to stop by sometime, he considered Dan, who hung back, staring at the ground, as if awaiting sentencing. Logan shoved his hands into his pockets, matching the boy's stance.

"You ready to go home?"

"You tell me. Is it my home?" the boy asked, looking up long enough to eye him skeptically.

"What kind of question is that? Yeah, it's your home. For as long as you want it. Always, if that appeals to you. Provided you stop scaring the hell out of your mother, and turning her inside out."

"Well, what about what she did to me?"

The question carried more pain than belligerence. Logan sighed. "What did she do to you, Dan? Carry you for nine months? Give birth to you and then spend the next fifteen years of her life worrying if you had enough food, clothes, love, to grow up to be a healthy, well-balanced kid? Wow, what a rotten deal, man."

"You're defending her because you hated my father," Dan said, clenching his hands at his sides.

"I don't hate your father. I resented his behavior quite a few times, I was disappointed in it even more often. Most of all," he added with no small amount of chagrin, "I was jealous that he got the girl I'd realized too late that I wanted. That's more than enough baggage to carry without adding hate to it."

"But he was a draft dodger, and you went to Vietnam. Don't tell me you didn't hate him for that."

"I was deeply disappointed in him because of the way he handled it." Logan shifted to lean against the tailgate of his truck. "And if he would have done it because of some deep philosophical commitment, I would have respected him—but he ran, Danny. What bothers me about it most, though, was that his decision profoundly affected you and your mom's quality of life."

"We were all right."

"If a man brings a child into this world, he owes him the best of himself. Remember that," Logan said. He had never been more serious. "'All right' isn't good enough. Your mother covered for your father, so that you wouldn't see his flaws, and would love and respect him. But the first time she does something for herself, what do you do? You insult her."

The boy's chin trembled, and he looked away. "Everything's changing. I don't know about anything anymore. I came into the house, and there she was packing away Dad's picture, and all his stuff."

"We need the room for a nursery, Dan. Regardless of how I felt toward your father before, I respect your mother's right to keep things of his for you. No one's going to tell you never to mention him. In fact, I think your grandmother would enjoy hearing you talk about the things you two did together a great deal. But life *is* change. Your dad had a problem facing that, and he ran. If you run, you'd better be ready to accept that it's very hard to stop."

Dan looked up at the sky. The air was cooling fast, and the T-shirt he was wearing, which had been adequate during the warm day, now left him wrapping his arms around himself and shaking. Logan wanted to give him his sport jacket, but knew he needed to get some kind of signal from the kid first.

"At first I thought about hitching my way back to Canada."

Knowing it would be a mistake to overreact to the boy's confession, Logan nodded. But his heart ached for Merri as he thought of all the heartache and tragedy that would have brought on. "It would have been a long, dangerous trip."

"Yeah. I thought I might need some more self-defense lessons, and maybe save some money, a bunch more money, before I ever started thinking in that line again."

He caught the boy's sidelong look, and knew they'd made it over the worst part of the ordeal. "Not an unwise decision. I know your mother worries about you being too interested in what she sees as activities promoting violence, but I'd be happy to talk to her about it, try to make her see it's a form of physical and mental exercise, then sign you up for whatever classes you'd like."

"You would?" Dan looked hopeful, but unconvinced. "I thought maybe, with the redecorating and new baby and stuff, money would be tight."

Logan hid a smile. "Well, I'll try not to brag, but I am fairly successful at what I do. I think we can squeeze in the lessons."

The boy ducked his head even more, but murmured his thanks. After a moment, a long, relieved sigh gushed out of him. "I, uh, guess we can head on home, don't you?"

"Absolutely."

Logan got choked up the moment they walked into the house and he saw Merri's expression. No sunrise ever had anything on her smile. She opened her arms to her son, and he rushed into them. When she looked at him over her boy's shoulder, the emotions he saw in those gorgeous eyes made him know with a certainty that he would do just about anything for her.

Since his mother demanded her hug from the boy, Logan didn't have to wait long to finally hold his wife. But he left the explanations up to Danny, and didn't say a word when the teen left a few embarrassing confessions out.

"It's over now," his grandmother said, sniffing. "And thank God, everyone's safe."

Merri simply held Logan tight and whispered, "Thank you."

She looked dead on her feet, and knowing that Dan needed rest, too, he suggested that since Mike LeBlanc had informed the authorities for them, they could turn in. He knew Merri would have stayed up longer to mother her son, but Logan had only to exchange one look with *his* mother to know that at least the feeding part of that nurturing would be taken care of.

Relieved, he wasted no time in getting his wife upstairs. In fact, halfway up and out of sight of the others, he lifted her into his arms and carried her the rest of the way.

"Logan...this is crazy," she whispered, but she was laughing, too. "I'm tired, not an invalid. Put me down."

Instead, he shut their bedroom door with a nudge of his foot. "I've been waiting all day to say this," he began, sitting down on the bed and settling her on his lap. "I wanted to say it last night, but you fell asleep. I meant to say it as soon as I got home this afternoon, but—"

"I love you, too."

He exhaled. "Always taking the wind out of my sails."

"I couldn't wait any longer for you to get to the point so I could say it myself." She pressed her cheek to his. "Of course, we already knew the truth."

"Yeah." But he'd waited a damn long time to feel the words on his tongue, and he intended to say them. "I love you, Merri."

Her arms tightened around his neck. For a long moment, she didn't move, didn't breathe, and he knew she was fighting tears. He knew that for the most part they were

:ears of exhaustion and relief, but he hoped a few were of
1appiness, too.

"Logan," she said at last, her voice suspiciously thick,
>ut happy, "we're so lucky. And I'm *so* proud of you."

"I told you, LeBlanc found him." As much as he en-
oyed the compliment, he wasn't about to deceive her.

"I'm proud because of who you are, of the man I real-
zed you'd become. You *are* a hero, Logan."

He had to shake his head at that. "Sweetheart, I don't
>elieve in heroes. Even when they gave me those medals
downstairs for saving my platoon leader's life and stuff, I
felt like a fraud. No, a thief. Hell, honey, you know what my
option was? I either reacted or I'd be dead, too.

"People use that word too easily. To me the people who
get called heroes are simply individuals who've lived up to
their capacity as human beings. Just the other day some ac-
tor said the same thing on a TV interview, and I thought,
es, there's someone who understands. We don't have to
give responsibility and caring special names to make people
pay attention and reach for the best in themselves. I knew
that as a soldier. I had to learn that as a civilian." He stroked
her cheek. "Do you know who taught me my last lessons?
You."

He kissed her then, because it was time; because he
needed it more than his next breath; because it was late and
they were both completely drained and there was no way on
earth anything more intimate was going to happen between
them tonight no matter how wonderful it would be.

What he forgot was what happened when he kissed Merri.

Sweet turned to serious faster than fire consumed tissue
paper. She moaned. He groaned. Jointly their hands began
to make forays, not just to caress, but to push aside clothing, as well.

Breaking for air, nose to nose with him, Merri looked into his eyes. "I could get a little crazy over you, Mr. Powers."

Remembering his words from last night, and then his thought of only moments ago, Logan broke into a slow, unabashed grin. "I'm willing."

Epilogue

The following summer

Merri blinked up at the new addition to the family residence, which was now being painted to match the rest of the white-and-blue structure. The two-story extension would be their wing of the house by next week. "Logan...it's so big."

"On the outside, maybe, but once Stan moves in and we put in the computer room for Dan, not to mention my office, you won't be saying that."

He was probably right, as usual. When it came to houses, she thought with a secret smile. Her smile broadened when she thought of Stan Shirley. His joining the family was the latest round of lovely news they'd received recently and she couldn't wait for his wedding to Faith, now that her mother-in-law had finally broken down and accepted his proposal.

But as Logan took the gurgling bundle from her arms, she knew her favorite "event" recently was their new son.

Nicholas James Powers was now three months old, and growing faster than the Powers homestead. As she watched Logan kiss the butterball's fisted hand, she sighed with gratitude.

While the rest of her pregnancy had been relatively without complications, her delivery had been a nightmare. Danny had broken his arm carrying her suitcase downstairs to the car; Logan had literally knocked a tire off the truck trying to get them both to the hospital. In the end, it had been Faith, following in her station wagon, who saved the day and the family from more catastrophe.

Faith... she was swinging on the garden swing that Stan had bought her as an early wedding present. Now that the postal carrier was retiring, he wanted his lady to spend more time enjoying life with him. Everyone was glad of that, and they were going to start by throwing a huge retirement party here next week. It would precede the couple's quiet family wedding a few days later. After a brief honeymoon to Branson, Missouri, the country-and-western hot spot that Stan had been dying to visit, Merri expected to see the winsome newlyweds smooching on that swing often.

As for Danny, he was off with Sherman, somewhere on the place. The two had been thick as thieves since school let out, and Logan had hinted that they were experimenting with an irrigation invention that would make hoses and wheel-driven contraptions obsolete. Whether or not that happened, she was incredibly proud of her firstborn. After that tricky start, he'd adapted so well to the whirlwind changes, and his respect and affection for Logan was very real.

Life couldn't be better.

Faith called for them to give Nicky to her so that they could stroll around the house more freely. Merri chuckled when Logan didn't hesitate. Their littlest angel was becoming quite a weighty bundle, and promising to be every bit as big and strong as his daddy.

Logan took her by the hand, but instead of circling the house to get the effect from a different angle, he led her to the stock pond, which had become a favorite spot since their marriage. "Remember how you dragged me out of here so many years ago?" she asked as she sank onto the lush grass minutes later.

"Yup, but you could reenact it if you want, so I can appreciate what you grew up to look like," he murmured, sprawling beside her.

"Flattery will get you into trouble," she teased.

"I'm trying as hard as I can."

She laughed and dropped onto her back to look up at the sky. "It's good, Logan. So good. Thank you."

He bent over her and kissed her tenderly. "It was your doing. You came back to me."

"Who would have known...?"

"We always knew."

He was right again. And she didn't mind one bit.

* * * * * *

COMING NEXT MONTH

MILLION DOLLAR SWEEPSTAKES (III)

No purchase necessary. To enter, follow the directions published. Method of entry may vary. For eligibility, entries must be received no later than March 31, 1996. No liability is assumed for printing errors, lost, late or misdirected entries. Odds of winning are determined by the number of eligible entries distributed and received. Prizewinners will be determined no later than June 30, 1996.

Sweepstakes open to residents of the U.S. (except Puerto Rico), Canada, Europe and Taiwan who are 18 years of age or older. All applicable laws and regulations apply. Sweepstakes offer void wherever prohibited by law. Values of all prizes are in U.S. currency. This sweepstakes is presented by Torstar Corp., its subsidiaries and affiliates, in conjunction with book, merchandise and/or product offerings. For a copy of the Official Rules send a self-addressed, stamped envelope (WA residents need not affix return postage) to: MILLION DOLLAR SWEEPSTAKES (III) Rules, P.O. Box 4573, Blair, NE 68009, USA.

EXTRA BONUS PRIZE DRAWING

No purchase necessary. The Extra Bonus Prize will be awarded in a random drawing to be conducted no later than 5/30/96 from among all entries received. To qualify, entries must be received by 3/31/96 and comply with published directions. Drawing open to residents of the U.S. (except Puerto Rico), Canada, Europe and Taiwan who are 18 years of age or older. All applicable laws and regulations apply; offer void wherever prohibited by law. Odds of winning are dependent upon number of eligibile entries received. Prize is valued in U.S. currency. The offer is presented by Torstar Corp., its subsidiaries and affiliates in conjunction with book, merchandise and/or product offering. For a copy of the Official Rules governing this sweepstakes, send a self-addressed, stamped envelope (WA residents need not affix return postage) to: Extra Bonus Prize Drawing Rules, P.O. Box 4590, Blair, NE 68009, USA.

SWP-S795

He's Too Hot To Handle...but she can take a little heat.

SILHOUETTE

Summer Sizzlers

This summer don't be left in the cold, join Silhouette for the hottest Summer Sizzlers collection. The perfect summer read, on the beach or while vacationing, Summer Sizzlers features sexy heroes who are "Too Hot To Handle." This collection of three new stories is written by bestselling authors Mary Lynn Baxter, Ann Major and Laura Parker.

Available this July wherever Silhouette books are sold.

SS95

COMING IN JULY FROM

SILHOUETTE®

Desire

THE DISOBEDIENT BRIDE
by Joan Johnston

book three of her bestselling

CHILDREN OF

series

Texas rancher Zach Whitelaw advertised for a wife to bear his children—but if she wasn't pregnant in a year's time, he'd divorce her! Six months into their marriage, Rebecca Littlewolf Whitelaw's tummy was as flat as on her wedding day. So, short of stuffing a pillow under her shirt, what was a wife in love supposed to do?

Don't miss THE DISOBEDIENT BRIDE in July...only from Silhouette Desire.

SDHW7

Three strong-willed Texas siblings whose rock-hard protective walls are about to come tumblin' down!

The Silhouette Desire miniseries by

BARBARA McCAULEY

continues with

August 1995

TEXAS TEMPTATION (Silhouette Desire #948)
Jared Stone had lived with a desperate guilt. Now he had a shot to make everything right again—until the one woman he couldn't have became the only woman he wanted.

Then read the conclusion in December 1995 with:

TEXAS PRIDE (Silhouette Desire #971)
Raised with a couple of overprotective brothers, Jessica Stone *hated* to be told what to do. So when her sexy new foreman started trying to run her life, Jessica's pride said she had to put a stop to it. But her heart said something *entirely* different....

And if you missed **TEXAS HEAT** (Silhouette Desire #917), the first book in the *Hearts of Stone* trilogy, be sure to order your copy today!

Rugged rancher Jake Stone had just found out that he had a long-lost half sister—and he was determined to get to know her. Problem was, her legal guardian and aunt, sultry Savannah Roberts, was intent on keeping him at arm's length.

As a
Privileged Woman,
you'll be entitled to all
these _Free Benefits._
And _Free Gifts,_ too.

To thank you for buying our books, we've designed an exclusive FREE program called _PAGES & PRIVILEGES™_. You can enroll with just one Proof of Purchase, and get the kind of luxuries that, until now, you could only read about.

_B_IG HOTEL DISCOUNTS

A privileged woman stays in the finest hotels. And so can you—at up to 60% off! Imagine standing in a hotel check-in line and watching as the guest in front of you pays $150 for the same room that's only costing you $60. Your _Pages & Privileges_ discounts are good at Sheraton, Marriott, Best Western, Hyatt and thousands of other fine hotels all over the U.S., Canada and Europe.

_F_REE DISCOUNT TRAVEL SERVICE

A privileged woman is always jetting to romantic places. When you fly, just make one phone call for the lowest published airfare at time of booking—or double the difference back! PLUS— you'll get a $25 voucher to use the first time you book a flight AND 5% cash back on every ticket you buy thereafter through the travel service!

SD-PP3A

*F*REE GIFTS!

A privileged woman is always getting wonderful gifts.
Luxuriate in rich fragrances that will stir your senses (and his). This gift-boxed assortment of fine perfumes includes three popular scents, each in a beautiful designer bottle. <u>Truly Lace</u>...This luxurious fragrance unveils your sensuous side. <u>L'Effleur</u>...discover the romance of the Victorian era with this soft floral. <u>Muguet des bois</u>...a single note floral of singular beauty.

YOURS FREE!

$50 VALUE

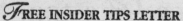

*F*REE INSIDER TIPS LETTER

A privileged woman is always informed. And you'll be, too, with our free letter full of fascinating information and sneak previews of upcoming books.

*M*ORE GREAT GIFTS & BENEFITS TO COME

A privileged woman always has a lot to look forward to. And so will you. You get all these wonderful FREE gifts and benefits now with only one purchase...and there are no additional purchases required. However, each additional retail purchase of Harlequin and Silhouette books brings you a step closer to even more great FREE benefits like half-price movie tickets... and even more FREE gifts.

L'Effleur...This basketful of romance lets you discover L'Effleur from head to toe, heart to home.

Truly Lace... A basket spun with the sensuous luxuries of Truly Lace, including Dusting Powder in a reusable satin and lace covered box.

Complete the Enrollment Form in the front of this book and mail it with this Proof of Purchase.

PROOF OF PURCHASE
Offer expires October 31, 1996

SD-PP3